Mixed Emotions

Mixed Emotions

L. M. Tinsley

TATE PUBLISHING
AND ENTERPRISES, LLC

Mixed Emotions
Copyright © 2015 by L. M. Tinsley. All rights reserved.

No part of this publication may be reproduced, stored in a retrieval system or transmitted in any way by any means, electronic, mechanical, photocopy, recording or otherwise without the prior permission of the author except as provided by USA copyright law.

This novel is a work of fiction. Names, descriptions, entities, and incidents included in the story are products of the author's imagination. Any resemblance to actual persons, events, and entities is entirely coincidental.

The opinions expressed by the author are not necessarily those of Tate Publishing, LLC.

Published by Tate Publishing & Enterprises, LLC
127 E. Trade Center Terrace | Mustang, Oklahoma 73064 USA
1.888.361.9473 | www.tatepublishing.com

Tate Publishing is committed to excellence in the publishing industry. The company reflects the philosophy established by the founders, based on Psalm 68:11,
"The Lord gave the word and great was the company of those who published it."

Book design copyright © 2015 by Tate Publishing, LLC. All rights reserved.
Cover design by Nikolai Purpura
Interior design by Jake Muelle

Published in the United States of America

ISBN: 978-1-63367-458-5
Fiction / Romance / General
14.11.19

To my family, I love you!

Acknowledgements

I would like to thank all of the friends and family that helped make *Mixed Emotions* possible.

First, I would like to extend gratitude to Beth King. Beth, your honest opinion and attention to details enriched my writing. I am honored to call you my friend and book confidant.

Next, I'd like to acknowledge my husband, Dave, and my son Memphis. I appreciate your support while I tackled this dream. I love you!

I would also like to acknowledge my friends, coworkers, and students—who allowed me to use your name or likeness as a muse in this creative process. Many of you read my early copies, submitted feedback, and took the time out of your lives to help make my manuscript complete. I cannot thank all of you enough.

Lastly, I would like to acknowledge my father. I thank God every day for the time I had with you and Dave's dad, Clay. I am even more thankful that He relieved both of you of your pain and allowed you to soar with the angels. Rest in peace.

1

Two months. Two months! "Are you serious?" Robert Taylor was shocked. Never had he imagined being in this position. Cancer. Really? Cancer. This could not be happening to him.

Sitting there in his doctor's office with his crystal blue eyes staring in disbelief at a pitifully painted brown wall, Robert ran his hand through his jet-black hair and shook his head to clear his thoughts. He didn't know if he should cry or burst out laughing. Instead, he just sat there stunned. Suddenly the walls started to creep in on him. He looked at his doctor, trying to hide the worry that was beginning to take hold. Questions began to form and jumble in his mind. When he spoke, he had to choose his words wisely to gain as much information as possible. He knew this disease meant certain death.

Dr. Marc Richardson sat across from Robert, re-examining the lab results he had ordered just a couple weeks earlier. As a rather ordinary but portly-looking man, Doc as Robert affectionately called him, was one of the foremost oncologists in the country. His medical discoveries were that of legend, and med students from all over the country studied his findings and memorized his techniques. He had graced the cover of all major medical magazines because of his forward thinking and aggressive research. This research made important people pay attention. Presidents chose him as their personal family oncologist. Stars flocked to him as their go-to man. Interestingly enough, all that fanfare had never mattered much to him. What mattered most were his patients.

When he telephoned Robert earlier that day, Doc had tried to hide the alarming concern in his voice. Even over the phone, he couldn't hold back the way he felt. Deep lines set between the doctor's bushy eyebrows. He couldn't remember the last time he'd called a patient personally to deliver any message, let alone discuss issues such as these. This time, however, was not just professional. It was personal. Robert deserved to hear the news face-to-face. He thought about that tense half hour he had waited for Robert to arrive. Doc knew he had given such news before, but for some reason, this hurt more than it used too.

Doc obviously hated this part of his job; it was written all over his face. His gray hair was thinning, and he sparsely had enough loose strands to comb over to the side—probably from the years of nervousness and worry for each and every patient. The spectacles on his troubled face magnified his deep chocolate eyes to comical proportions. Robert thought back to the times as a young child when he had been in this office, each time with a different member of his family. He had pointed at those large eyes more times than he could count, smiling and reaching up to the happily grinning man. Robert had always thought those memories were

Mixed Emotions

unique. They hid the troubling times of loss and despair. Times where his family had become ill, plagued with the same cancer that was now affecting Robert too.

Robert was shocked and sat staring at the old man, not believing what he had just heard. He knew his jaw hung agape. He hadn't felt great lately, but he never imagined cancer was the cause. Somehow he managed to utter, "How can that be?"

Dr. Richardson shook his head. "Robert, this is serious. It's stage four cancer. Right now I believe it's isolated in the pancreas. We need to begin treatment as soon as possible."

As a doctor, he had to separate himself from his relationship as Robert's friend and give him the facts. Doc settled into his well-practiced speech. "Robert, you know better than anyone how difficult something like this can be. No one has survived this disease without a fierce battle. It is aggressive and for many incurable. My heart aches right now, just as I am sure yours does too. I have always looked at you as one of my own. Your family has become part of mine. I encourage you to think about this carefully. You need to prepare your family and affairs. As you have experienced firsthand, there isn't much time to delay."

Robert looked at Doc in total defeat, his mouth opening and closing, but the words were hard-pressed to come out. "There has to be something we can do. Please, Doc, tell me." He was practically begging for a lifeline. Something tangible that could keep his head above water.

Doc looked at Robert and took a deep breath. He steadied himself. His voice gained bravado as he began, "There is a treatment option I think will be best, but it's only in the trial stages right now."

Robert didn't care; he would try anything. He felt the tunnel of darkness quickly surrounding him. A deathtrap restraining him and having no end in sight, no solid hope to be found. How was he ever going to make it through this illness?

His troubled thoughts were interrupted as Doc continued. "Pactinal is an experimental drug that uses your own blood cells as a tool to reprogram the immune system. This process is said to jump-start those blood cells and heal the problem areas. All of the studies, thus far, show an eighty-nine percent success rate. It extends a patient's life and has been known to cure people within one six-week treatment cycle."

Robert didn't know what to say. How would he be able to get this treatment and live a productive life? His family consumed his thoughts. Loss had filled his childhood. Memories of a broken family still ached him after all this time. He knew the horror stories; he had lived them. "How long will I be down, Doc? I have my work to think of and my family."

Doc smiled at Robert's concern for his family. Amazingly, he wasn't thinking about himself, even though it was all about him. "Look, Robert, you are one of the lucky ones." Doc needed to put things into perspective for him. He hoped to sway Robert to take him seriously about this treatment. It could mean the difference between life and death.

Sure, Robert thought to himself, *I'm the one dying here. My wife and kids will be the ones affected.* "How can I possibly be lucky?" Robert asked despairingly.

Doc looked at Robert with awe. He'd never thought Robert a skeptic of his treatment success nor of his own body's resilience. Doc forged ahead with continued optimism. "Thank goodness it doesn't require a port to administer. A port just complicates the access point with infections. And oral medications, well, oral meds just keep you sick for days upon days."

What Doc had said did make sense to him, but Robert just couldn't put it all together. His thoughts cycled between grief, desperation, and despair. He needed time. He needed space. Something. He just didn't know what.

"Take a day to think about it. Call me anytime day or night. Ask me as many questions as you need. I will administer the treatment myself during my OSU Medical Center rounds," Doc stated. "You know I'll be there for you every step of the way."

Robert conceded to think about Doc's recommendation. Although he didn't have much time, he wanted to make the best choice for him and his family. As he left Doc's office with his death sentence looming over his head, he was tired and frustrated. What would he tell his wife and kids? Should he tell them or let them be unaware? One moment he seemed to have the answer. The next moment he didn't. He knew it wasn't going to be an easy decision.

The prescribed treatment was experimental at best and, even though Doc hadn't mentioned it, could probably cause severe side effects. He was just forty-five.

For goodness' sake, he was dying. *This was ridiculous!* He drove his modest sedan down E. Town St. and turned on Third. Maybe he should head down Fourth to Broad St. or take a walk in the Short North. Maybe walk off a short pier? Robert truly didn't know what he should do.

2

Alexandria Taylor danced around the kitchen listening to Rascal Flatts on her bright-green-covered iPhone. She had been gathering ingredients for an exquisite dinner. She sashayed high and low reaching in and around cabinets. Of course, many of the items she needed were high up on the shelf.

Alex looked around to see what was available to use. She'd have to get a pair of tongs or a long ladle to get them down. She puffed up her bangs that had precariously fallen into her eyes with an exasperated breath. When you're five foot, this is a regular occurrence. She sighed and said to herself, "Who needs to work out? It's like a gymnastics routine just trying to get something off the top shelves."

She grabbed the long ladle and swatted the last of the seasonings down. She didn't realize one was heading right for her head. It fell with a thud right between her eyes. "Seriously? Ouch," she yelled, rubbing the bridge of her nose between her eyes.

As she looked on the ground for the offending spice, she grimaced. "Ugh." She hated being small. Hopefully the rest of the preparation would be less—dangerous.

She smiled to herself; a little bit of red wine would help things too.

She looked at the bright-blue digital clock illuminating from the stove and wondered when Robert would be home. He hadn't been at the office this afternoon, and she had eventually taken a cab.

Although initially, she was mad that he hadn't told her he was leaving, she hoped they could have a quiet dinner together. The kids had been busy with their lives, and they hadn't called or come over in days. She thought just reconnecting with her husband after a painfully long day would be a much-needed distraction. But when dinner was ready, Robert was still not home. She didn't want the food to get cold, so she resolved to start eating. Turning off the music and turning on the TV, Alex set up a small tray table and sank down on the dark-chocolate suede couch. Since Robert wasn't home yet, she hoped maybe one of the *Housewives of Somewhere* would give her a little company.

After eating, she left a mess in the kitchen, too despondent to clean. Alex didn't care if the kitchen stayed dirty, a thought that surprised her since she usually was a complete and total neat freak. She leaned back with a full and content stomach and swiftly drifted off into a restless sleep. It was hours later before she heard Robert come stumbling through the door.

⁂

Robert noticed Alex's sleepy eyes watching him from the couch as he opened the door, but he didn't acknowledge she was there. He didn't want to talk; he felt terrible. He knew she probably had a million questions.

At the moment, Robert couldn't dare to approach the subject. He dismissed the calls she'd placed to his smartphone without another thought. In his heart, he knew more than anything her probable discontent at being sent right to voice mail. She'd just have to be frustrated. Honestly, she had no idea about actual frustration. True frustration would be realizing you have no idea what to say to the love of your life each time she called.

Feeling so overcome with the previous news, he made himself at home in the Hyatt Hotel's bar having a few drinks and talking to an empathetic bartender. He'd have to go back to get his car in the morning.

Even though Robert was sick, he didn't feel the need to die any earlier by driving drunk. He thought about his dilemma. The hardest part of this terrible situation was the fact he knew the truth. What was happening would break Alex's heart. With one frustrated breath, he quickly retreated to their bedroom. Robert didn't even give her a chance to utter a word. "Hi to you too, dear," he heard as he went into their bedroom.

As he closed the door behind him, Robert noticed she'd decided not to follow. She must really be pissed. Pissed he could deal with, breaking her heart he couldn't. Frankly, it sickened him to think about the medical trial and error ahead. If he didn't tell her about the experimental drugs or treatments, would she think something else was going on? Maybe he should help ease the pain and just tell her? "Ridiculous!" Robert scolded himself as he loosened the tie that already felt like a noose hanging around his neck. Death was knocking at his door. He couldn't tell her, or was it more like he *wouldn't* tell her. At least, he couldn't right now.

He moved around the plush master bedroom, and he weighed the pros and cons. The more he thought about it, a family, an amazing, loving family was about to be shaken to its core. No ordinary plan of action would work here. Robert was desperate.

Instantly, a brilliant yet devious plan began to form in Robert's mind. Money, he needed money. Money solved problems. In the back of his mind, however, his conscience urged him not to be too hasty in his decisions. Robert just shrugged. If all else failed, his plan just might work.

3

Alex looked around. *Interesting*, she thought. *I don't remember coming in here.* She had to laugh. With the way she drank the wine last night, she wasn't surprised at her apparent amnesia. She groaned and grunted as the speakers on her alarm blared, "It's *five* o'clock somewhere." Of course, Jackson and Buffet had no worries! Alex grumbled, "Why would they?" The two superstars had earned millions of dollars by singing in support of adult beverages. Interestingly enough, she didn't want to hear about it this early in the morning, especially since she wasn't a millionaire and had a job where she needed to be in about an hour.

Even though she hadn't even crawled out of bed yet, nor had the day reached 8:00 a.m., here at home, Alex assessed from the throbbing in her head that it wasn't going to be a day she would want to sing about, let alone one to toast.

As she pushed the button to stop the incessant alarm noise, she realized the spot next to her was cold. Robert must have left for work earlier. His nightstand was clear of the personal effects he always kept on him, a telltale sign he was still home. "Ugh! Great," she moaned to herself. "And I'll have to go work alone."

She threw off her cocoon of covers and decided she better get ready for work. Of course, she'd have to take some aspirin and make herself some coffee before she left, anything to help ease the pounding in her head. Shortly thereafter, Alex realized it wasn't going to be that easy. As her luck would have it, she couldn't find keys to the other car. Stomping her foot, she shouted, "Seriously! Why does this crap always happen to me?"

Alex started to dial Robert's number but, after looking at the clock, realized it was too late. Robert wouldn't be able to do anything, which left her no other option, but to catch the bus. She practically had to run to get to it on time, managing to fall only once. She hadn't any coffee and was still nursing quite a headache from the indulgence of wine. Too bad her knees hadn't fared well either; she was scraped up and bleeding on both.

As Alex sat down on an empty seat to the right of the bus, she tended to her wounds with a random Dairy Queen napkin she had found at the bottom of her purse. She spent out a harsh breath and huffed to no one in particular. "My hair is crazy, my head hurts, and I just want to get to work!"

She peered up to see an old and wrinkly man looking at her, a look of amusement on his aged face. She shrugged her shoulders and gave him a half-smile. He turned his head and covered his mouth with his long wrinkly fingers. Alex was sure he was trying to stifle a laugh as he viewed her disheveled state. *Nice*, she thought to herself.

She reached back into her purse and was pleased to find a hair tie in a side pocket. When Alex looked down at her discovery, a giggle escaped before she even realized it. In her hand, she held the hair tie, a paper clip, piece of gum, and a sticky note to buy milk. She looked up to find the man's eyes had met hers once again. She held out the gum and offered it to the man; he declined with a shake of his head. *His loss,* she thought. She shrugged and threw the extra findings back into her purse.

Alex smoothed the wispy pieces of hair that fell in her eyes as best as she could with her right hand as she flipped the rest of her hair up to secure it in the tie with her left. It was the best she could do without a comb. *Oh well,* she thought to herself. *It could always be worse.*

Finally, the bus came to a stop outside her office building. Alex looked out the window and noticed the workers hanging a new "Monroe, Clayton, and Davidson, LLC" sign. Mr. Whinehart, her boss, was set to arrive any day now, and the office was abuzz preparing for his return from abroad. *Good thing he isn't going to be here today,* she thought. She knew seeing him or anybody else was out of the question. When Alex stood up and met the old man's eyes once again, he nodded with an astute look. It was as if he knew exactly what she was thinking. She laughed, and he probably agreed.

❧

"What on earth is wrong with you?" Alex looked up to find her dearest friend and colleague, Tamara Drawn, staring at her in disgust. Obviously her disheveled state was *alarming.*

She rubbed the back of her neck. It was all kinked from first falling asleep on the couch. She wished she would have thought about moving to her bed a little earlier, but it was late—well early in the morning when she finally had. Could it possibly be the residual effects of the wine? Maybe the *entire* bottle had been a little too much.

Tamara noticed her friend had thrown her hair haphazardly in a ponytail. The typical waterfall of Alex's long black hair usually cascaded down her creamy-white skin, but today, not so much. She wasn't even sure Alex had put on any makeup, not that she needed it. Her friend's eyes rivaled any jade statue the Far East produced or traded. No matter her age, Alex was a beauty.

The morning had not been kind to her friend, and Tamara could tell. Alex's eyes were puffy and red. It occurred to her something else was off too. Then it hit her! What in the world was she wearing? She generally dressed well, all-be-it modestly. Tamara appreciated how Alex always tried to experiment with style, colors, and comfort. *Not so much today…* Tamara thought to herself.

It was evident from the expression on her face that Alex was not in the mood this morning, not even for her best friend. Tamara, however, could not let her walk around looking like this. "Alex," she said in the most lovingly and sarcastic voice possible. "Did you totally not look in the mirror this morning?"

Alex shrugged her shoulders as she tilted her head to the side. She looked pathetic and utterly bewildered. Tamara laughed. "You are so lucky I like you and can get over this horrid appearance."

Alex just rolled her eyes. "Really? Why's that?"

Tamara stood then walked around the side of her desk and toward Alex. "Alex, honey, did you see that your shoes don't match?"

Alex shrieked as she looked at her feet. "WHAT?"

Tamara laughed out loud. This *was* bad. "Let's go into your office," she said. "Don't you have a change of shoes and maybe some clothes in there?"

Alex just nodded and leaned onto her friend. Tamara put her arm around her shoulders. She whispered just above Alex's ear, "Hopefully you have a hairbrush in there too."

꩜

Unfortunately, the options available in Alex's office were limited. "I cannot wear my gym shoes around the office. I do have some dignity." Alex sighed.

Tamara had to laugh. "Really, dignity?" she continued sarcastically. "I totally observed that when you came in."

Alex knew she had a point. She was originally wearing two different shoes. The sneakers were just going to have to do for today. She decided, "I could just hide in my office as long as an important client isn't on the schedule."

Tamara nodded. Was Alex so bad off that she couldn't even seem to remember today's appointments? Routine and schedule, order and structure, those were Alex's crutches. What was wrong with her? Tamara determined it was going to be a long day for poor Alex!

A knock on the office door had indicated Alex's assistant before he stuck his skinny yet pointed head into her office. Tamara decided that was her cue to leave.

She smiled at Alex and gave a sympathetic wave while walking out the door.

※

Someone in the MCD Human Resources Department had a sense of humor. That was the only reason Alex could fathom why her new assistant, Albert Barnes, was even hired. Or, he was a friend of a friend's son. Who knew?

Alex mostly worked with her husband and just wasn't doing well with the change. She thought she was doing fine, then this kid showed up. She normally was so good with people that Mr. Whinehart had asked she train and supervise the interns. Unfortunately, Albert seemed to rub her the wrong way. He was smug, arrogant, and continuously a thorn in her curvy side.

Barely twenty-five years old and still living at home, Albert Barnes was your typical momma's boy wrapped up in a pink polo shirt and blue Dockers pants. His brown loafers squeaked atop the floor. The moment he spoke, Alex felt as though someone was scraping his or her fingernails down an old chalkboard. Today was ten times worse.

Albert pushed his thick black glasses up on his nose. They always seemed to be falling down. "Whoa, Alex!" And just like that, his nasally voice whistled its way into the room. "You okay? You look terrible!"

Alex wanted to scream. *What is with you, people?* Once again, Alex puffed her bangs out of her eyes as she glared at him. Then closing her eyes, she took in a deep breath before she spoke. "Yes, Albert. What can I do for—"

"Mr. Taylor called earlier." As always, Albert forged ahead with what he had to say, ignoring the fact that Alex was even speaking. Although usually a nuisance, his news was not all that bad. Finally, Albert began to turn around and leave just as quickly as he had come. Alex realized she had bent toward her desk, bracing for the ear-piercing noise that emanated from Albert. Holding on to the edge of her desk like her life depended on it, Alex realized her knuckles were turning white. She released her fingers and allowed the blood to flow back into each one. Maybe she had gotten lucky today, and he wasn't interested in talking to her? *Not so painful*, she thought.

As he started to walk out, Alex realized he wasn't quite done. He turned his head and lifted his chin as he shouted out behind him, "Oh, and Mr. Whinehart is here. He wants to see you now."

Alex responded just the way Albert had hoped. Her face drained and became almost white. From the looks of it, she probably wasn't prepared for a meeting with the boss this morning. Albert smiled a Cheshire-cat smile as Alex sunk down in her chair in utter defeat.

This was getting ridiculous! Alex needed to get her self together, figure out whatever was going on with her boss, and begin her work. *Well*, Alex thought, *I might as well get started with my day.* She stood up, straightened her skirt, and smoothed back her loose strands of hair. Holding her head up high, she walked out of her office.

She waved good-bye to her ever-nosy friend, who was precariously hiding behind a magazine (which Alex could see was completely upside down), and pushed passed her newly appointed nemesis's desk. She'd call Robert later. She had to deal with her boss right now. Alex scurried down the office corridor ignoring her other coworkers. Her mind was on all the things she had to do today. As she rounded the corner, she ran smack-dab into an immovable object.

4

Walter Messenger wandered around the seemingly endless hallways of Monroe, Clayton, and Davidson, LLC searching for his new office. He had been transferred to Ohio from California, and he seemed a million miles away from anything resembling home. He was tall, good-looking, athletic, and well-educated. The all-American type of guy: blond hair, blue eyes, and all muscle. First in his class at UCLA and now part of a lucrative business, life was good and simple. He liked things that way. As he fumbled with his banker's box and coffee cup, he didn't seem to notice that someone was rapidly coming around the corner.

There wasn't any time to move. As he dodged an opening office door, he ran smack-dab into the little tornado. Startled, a petite rather attractive woman looked up to find a coffee-soaked Walter.

"Oh, I'm so sorry!" she said. "I wasn't looking up. Gosh, I didn't know you were there. Are you hurt?"

He flashed what he had been told was his women-swoon-over-me smile. Then she slapped her hands over her mouth. A small squeak came from behind her hand. Walter thought, *Was that a giggle? She was giggling?*

Right then, Walter's cheeks turned bright red. *Not quite the response I was hoping to receive.*

Of course, now the coffee was dripping down off the top of his head and into his eyes. He realized it *was* kind of funny and not in the least bit attractive. *Well, maybe he'd go with humor.* He managed to mutter, "I'm good. Soggy but good." He looked down at the soaked box of files and his shirt. The woman gestured and then led him to what must have been her office space. He followed behind her with his bruised ego partially intact.

Walter sat his box on the office chair and watched as she pulled a hand towel out of her gym bag already sitting on her desk. "I promise, it's clean," she said after seeing his eyes wander down to the bag. He took the towel out of her hand and started to wipe himself off. While brushing off his shirt, he couldn't keep his mind from wondering, *How am I ever going to recover from this?*

As he looked back up at the raven-haired beauty, he realized she was staring at him. Walter hoped he wasn't drooling or something. That would be just his luck. The coffee stain on his clothes and in his hair was bad enough. He wiped down his head and face. Then he rubbed the towel down the legs of his pants. Finally, he handed the lovely woman back her towel.

She sat it down on her solid mahogany desktop then put out her right hand and said, "Oh, I'm Alexandria Taylor." Her bright-green eyes took his breath away. He just stared. She continued and her hand faltered a little. "Well, most people just call me Alex. You are?"

Walter clasped her hand into his. "Walter Messenger." He stood tall and puffed out his chest. If he tried, he could save himself some face. "Well, Alex, it looks as we've made one heck of an impression on each other, huh?" Her smile was infectious. Walter was relieved. His embarrassment was overshadowed by her kindness. He decided to tease her a little more. "You know I really do like coffee, Alex, but if it makes you feel better, I'll skip it from now on."

Alex had to laugh. "Well, I did hear caffeine is bad for your health. I'm really just saving your life." She was cool, calm, and collected, but Walter noticed she still couldn't help but have a huge smile. Sarcastic too, huh? He liked that.

Walter returned the charm with laughter. "Well, Alex, I can honestly say that this is a first for me. Thank you for your concern, but I promise you next time, I'll step away from the coffeepot." He was enjoying this moment. It wasn't long before he had lost his train of thought. *What exactly was he supposed to be doing?* When a cough happened behind him, he realized he was supposed to be going to Mr. Whinehart's office and not flirting like a teenager with raging hormones.

5

Robert looked at his Cartier watch Alex had bought him for their anniversary. It was so extravagant, and he knew she had paid a fortune for the piece. He smiled at the thought of her face as she watched him open the box. So proud, so loving, and the most thoughtful woman he had ever known. Robert knew he was probably on his wife's bad side this morning because he had rushed out of the house before she even got out of bed. He never dreamed she'd bring their marital problems into the office. She hadn't even called him back.

Robert shook off his daydream; he only had about five minutes. He was due in Whinehart's office, so he went ahead and put his thoughts about Alex to the side. Then he rounded the corner to her office, and he was surprised to see a rather large blond man blocking the doorway. Robert let out a small cough, hoping to get his wife's attention and find out who exactly was in his wife's office.

Alex peered around Walter's broad shoulders and looked straight into her husband's eyes. He *had* to pick this exact moment to appear! She was standing in her office with another man who was soaking wet with coffee. At least Walter had gotten a chance to wipe off.

Unfortunately, her husband did not look away, and then his brows furrowed. *Crap*, she thought. "Oh, hi!" Alex said as nonchalantly as possible. She walked around Walter, and he turned to look at her as she walked by. He was now looking back and forth between her and her husband. She realized he must have been as surprised as she was by Robert's sudden appearance.

Robert looked questioningly at Alex. He said, "Uh, Alex, do you have a minute?" Before she could speak, Robert's eyes trailed up and down Walter's body. She knew he had to ask, but hoped he didn't.

"Hey, man, what's all over you?" Robert asked Walter. *Of course he did*, Alex thought.

Walter stood up tall. He wiped off the last few drops of coffee like he had just come out of a quick spring rain. He followed Robert's eyes and looked down at his shoes. He realized the coffee was not only on his shirt and pants but on his shoes too.

Robert saw Alex point to the coffee cup on the floor next to Walter's feet. Robert chuckled. Alex was never graceful. He guessed this man found out the hard way.

Walter couldn't help but notice the familiarity between Alex and this man. "You must be Mr. Taylor," he said, sticking his hand out for a handshake. "Alex was just defending me from the harmful effects of coffee and caffeine. I'm Walter Messenger. How do you do?"

Robert accepted Walter's hand with a hearty handshake. He looked at Walter and seemed to nod knowingly. He said, "Yes, she is thoughtful that way." His smile was friendly, and Walter was glad. This could have gone very badly if this guy was say, the jealous type.

He definitely had an amazing wife, one who was so beautiful and, well, seemed—*perfect*.

Alex looked at Walter and said, "Robert is Mr. Whinehart's right-hand man. He doesn't like to admit that, but it's true." Robert seemed flattered by her comment. He looked lovingly at his wife.

Walter could tell that their relationship was comfortable. Alex continued, "We met here over twenty years ago and haven't been apart since." Then she sighed. As she smiled back up at her husband, Walter couldn't help but notice the smile did not reach her eyes. He saw the slight hesitation, a rather unexpected response from what he thought was a happily married woman.

Then Walter picked up the conversation once again. "I'm in from the Sacramento office and was just getting ready to meet with Mr. Whinehart. Are you heading that way as well?" He held his hand out, allowing the couple to pass. They fell in side by side and started down the hallway with Walter behind them.

Something was bothering Alex, but of course, he tried not to get involved in his coworker's personal lives. Walter learned a long time ago to never intrude upon another's privacy. He didn't even know Alex, but Walter couldn't help but be drawn to her. Robert seemed not to notice her small hesitation before. Maybe it was nothing, or maybe it was everything. Walter intended to find out.

6

At forty-five years old, Julius Whinehart was one of the youngest CEOs of a Fortune 500 company. His black slicked-back hair and dark-blue suit was a stark contrast to his bright-blue eyes. His fit body could easily be detected under his designer clothes. He was tough but fair and had a keen eye for business. Julius was considered rather handsome and utterly irresistible to the women in the office. Robert was glad the frugal entrepreneur had not impressed his wife. She was all class and not influenced in any way by Julius's good looks.

Of course, Robert wasn't bad-looking himself. He was a tall dark-haired man with strong cheekbones and a physique that most men would sacrifice to have even at half his age. Alex knew the first time she saw him that she was going to become his wife. He felt it too.

Robert thought of that memory with fondness. He remembered how he at first turned down Julius's request to come in to the Midwest office. The only reason he had flown into Ohio from New York was just to meet a new client. Interestingly enough, Alex had been chosen to be his company liaison. As luck would have it, he was quite taken with her even though she was five years his junior. She made him feel at home.

One brief encounter led to wild, passionate love. It was a start to a long and beautiful relationship. The business trip for him became a permanent move for true love.

☙❧

Robert opened the door to Julius's corner office and allowed Alex to pass before him. He smiled once again, thinking how one decision had made a tremendous impact on his life. Little did he know that Walter had felt the exact same way too.

The view of the Columbus skyline was amazing, and the furnishings in Julius's office were the best of the best. Sleek lines, dark woods, and bright pops of color alluded to the hint of authority and decorator-like style. Julius was sitting at his desk combing over the reports Robert had submitted earlier. His brows were down, and he didn't seem pleased.

☙❧

Alex could tell Robert was anxious about the reports Julius was studying, but she couldn't understand why. Robert's work was always impeccable. He had no reason to be worried. She had looked over the reports on her own and was pleased with his findings. Profits were up, and the company was on track for even more success this quarter.

The sun shone on her husband's face, and to be honest, he didn't look well. It wasn't just something bothering him. In this light, he truly looked—unhealthy. It had to be his night of whatever he was doing to make him look that way. This made her remember being mad at him. Well, she wasn't letting him off that easy. She had work to do. She headed to the conference table. Walter was right behind her.

Robert wasn't looking forward to this meeting. He felt uncomfortable. It was time he told Julius the truth about his condition, but he couldn't do it with his wife or a new man in the room. Unfortunately, it would have to wait until later. Hopefully, it wouldn't be too much later; he didn't exactly know if he'd make it as many days as Doc projected.

Robert was definitely anxious about this difficult conversation. Hopefully, Alex wasn't figuring out he intended to tell Julius something he hadn't intended on telling her. He shifted his eyes to look at her. She looked back at him with an almost quizzical look. *Was she able to detect the ache and illness he had been feeling more and more lately?*

God, how he wished she could help him. Even if she was scared of the outcome, she could help him through whatever was happening. Robert knew she had made that vow a long time ago and was always bound and determined to stand behind it.

Walter watched the two of them and realized Alex was seeing something she hadn't noticed before. Robert came over to the table and sat on the empty chair next to him. They all sat quietly and waited for Julius to speak.

As Julius rose from his seat, Walter turned to look at him. He was glad his old friend had called and asked for his help in the Columbus office. It meant he had made an impression with all his hard work out in Sacramento. It also meant that something was not right in this office or completely missing altogether.

Julius looked at his newly formed team. He had waited a long time to have the three of them together, and it was finally time to expand the company internationally. Julius walked to the edge of the conference table, leaning forward as his hands cupped along the sides. He began to address them poignantly. "I want to first welcome Walter to our team. He is an amazing asset for us to have here and just the person we need to take our products and services global."

Walter realized now what his friend was trying to accomplish. He wanted to make MCD one of the foremost advertising firms in the world. It would be simple enough for them to accomplish with their impressive list of clients and amazing support staff. He knew the four of them together would be almost unstoppable.

Julius continued, "I find myself at a point where we either do this or we will no longer be profitable. We will have more than one task to accomplish together. First, we need to market ourselves to all the top businesses all round the world. Next, we need to gain their attention and make them want to be part of our firm. Last, we need to take them places no other company could have possibly imagined."

Robert, Alex, and Walter sat quietly thinking about what Julius was saying. Robert spoke first, "I think this is an excellent plan, and we need to get on it right away. Alex can find the most profitable businesses and contact their market-research departments. Walter, what exactly is your background?"

Walter didn't have an opportunity to answer because Julius spoke before he could. "Walter is an expert in the international marketplace. He has an extensive background in gaining the trust of major companies and enticing them to come on board. I want him fully involved with this process. Get used to each other because you are going to be spending a lot of time together."

༄

"You could have given me a heads-up, Jules." Walter looked at his friend after he took a drink out of his tumbler of bourbon. He had stayed at MCD hours after he had planned just to make sure he could wrap his hands around the ideas his new "partners" had disseminated. Robert and Alex had left an hour before, and he had just finished putting the gathered information into his portfolio. It was time he got the truth from his friend.

Julius raised his perfectly arched eyebrow and turned toward Walter. He said, "I have no idea what you're talking about." *Coy, real coy*, Walter thought. "I needed you for a project, so I called you in," Julius continued.

Walter knew that Julius had more planned, but he just hadn't told him exactly what yet. There was always more when it came to Julius. He leaned back on the long sleek-black couch in Julius's office. He tucked the bright-orange pillow under his arm. He'd better get comfortable because he wasn't leaving until he got the truth. "What's really going on here, Julius?"

Julius was looking back through his high-rise window at the beautifully lit downtown Columbus skyline. He said, "Walter, I want this company to be big, bigger than all of the other advertising companies out there not only in Ohio, but this nation. The only way to do that in the way I want is with you!"

He hadn't turned around to show he acknowledged the insinuation in Walter's question, but his answer hit at exactly what Walter had assumed. Walter adjusted his seat on the couch; he knew this determination. At times, this determination had gotten Julius in trouble. Fortunately, or unfortunately, Walter had always been around to see it firsthand.

As Julius turned to look at him, he realized his friend was in full business mode. "What *exactly* does that mean?" Walter said.

Julius smiled. "Just as I said, Walter. You are the brains that launched and marketed the Miller's Straw Pillow for the love of God! Who knew that the public wanted to sleep on a bunch of horse hay?"

Walter rolled his eyes. He interjected, "Straw, not hay. There *is* a difference." He had heard that enough in every meeting he'd ever held with that company. He'd probably hear it in his sleep.

"Whatever, it doesn't matter." Julius huffed. "It was genius of you to come up with that crazy slogan. What was it again?"

Walter would never forget it. "It's good for the horses and even better for you!" he mimicked in his best infomercial voice.

Julius laughed but got right back to his thought. "Right! It was genius! That's what I need for this project. Lawsonamto and Currbolinsaki want this toy to hit the American market by storm before Christmas. They gave us the privilege of presenting it to our market, and *we* are going to deliver. It's going to be bigger than Barbie!"

Walter was exasperated. He sighed and said, "I don't think the American market is ready for a geisha Barbie doll." Julius didn't even hear him through his delusional hype.

❦

Walter sat at his new downtown condo overlooking the Scioto River. The night was almost completely black except for the unnatural glow coming off the buildings of downtown Columbus. His restlessness made him feel almost caged.

Boxes were everywhere. Since today's events had kept Walter and took so much longer than expected, he didn't even have time to unpack one of them. Unfortunately, his work here was going to be as time-consuming as it was in California. He sighed. "Did I make a mistake?"

The sky was gray, not blue. The river was quiet, not alive. He longed for the sounds and movement of the ocean waves. The brightest of sunsets reflecting off the endless blue plain. That was home. Not this. This was—blah.

It wasn't the move that got to him; it was the loneliness. Walter's loneliness crept into his heart at the late hours of the night when work was finished, and the emptiness overtook his mind. He hadn't been in a fulfilling relationship in a long time. Even though he didn't have anyone but his brother back home, he had many friends and an active social life. The evenings were filled with after-hours bar trips and club nightlife.

Walter liked not thinking about the last time he was in love; he always had something, or more like someone, to occupy his thoughts.

He crossed through his spacious living room and walked to the custom-made wet bar. He poured himself a hearty glass of bourbon and brought it to his mouth. He savored the warmth as it slid down his throat. Walter walked over and smiled as he sat down and stretched out on his couch. It was then he thought back on what he considered the good years.

It was like a fairytale. True love had knocked on Walter's door his freshman year of college. Literally.

Shannon King was seeking donations for the homeless by selling Anthony Thomas chocolate bars. The passion she had for community service was all-encompassing, and Walter couldn't help but buy almost every candy bar she had in her bag. He took this chance encounter as an opportunity to learn more about this beautiful girl. Walter could tell from her quick humor and comebacks that she had a feisty redhead side too.

After five years of being constantly by her side, Walter had decided he wanted her to be his wife. He had worked and saved for months to purchase the most perfect diamond set in platinum. It took him days to plan the proposal. He could still feel the utter disbelief of her saying no.

Shannon was gone in a matter of months after that fateful night. Walter still ached each time he thought of her. It took him years before he realized she purposely said no to put distance between the two of them. It was obviously too difficult for her to tell him she was sick. As he lay his head against the back of the couch, it wasn't long before he drifted into a restless sleep. He was lost in the remembered depths of her deep-green eyes. Was it déjà vu that he'd met another jade-eyed beauty? Fate? To be honest, it was just his bad luck.

༺༻

The next morning, when he was getting ready for work, Walter laughed as he thought of his haphazard encounter with Alexandria Taylor. She was startled when she realized he was directly in her path. Then of course she couldn't help but sneak in a little joke—albeit at his expense.

He hadn't realized he'd be working with a woman. He thought, well, he thought she was a guy. No one mentioned *he* was a *she*. No one told him she would be a knockout. Alex. She was amazing, simply amazing. How interesting was it that his new coworker had the same shockingly green-colored eyes as the love of his life once had?

It was then Walter realized something was bugging him. He didn't know what it was. Eventually, after some deep thought, he realized the problem would be working with her so closely all the time. Well that, and her husband too.

7

Robert stared at the ceiling. It had been a restless night. He needed some time to think before he went into the office. It had only been a week since he received the news from Doc, and he wasn't sleeping. He hadn't since he found out. Right now his stomach hurt, and he ached all over. Robert was hiding from the truth, and he knew it.

It had been late in the evening when he got in, and Alex was not awake. Even though he tried to convince himself he had work at the office, in actuality, he wanted to slip in after she went to sleep. At first, he thought, *No questions. No answers.* Really, he had to face the fact he was acting like a coward.

Unfortunately, it just didn't matter. Sleep evaded him, *and* he missed kissing his wife good night. If he kept up like this, he would miss out on so many precious moments. Moments he didn't really have left to waste. As he blinked his restless eyes to the early light of dawn, he realized the lack of sleep tangled once again with troubling thoughts.

Robert's mind seemed to scramble as he began to think of options. God, he was back to the same questions over and over again: whether or not he should tell Alex or their children, if telling his boss would have negative affects. Would going in this alone give him the opportunity to fully allow himself to beat this disease? *Ugh!* No matter what, he hated just lying here. It didn't seem productive whatsoever.

It seemed as if hours had gone by when Robert finally rolled over and looked at Alex, but it had only been a few minutes. She began to stir, and he moved just a little to allow her to stretch. He couldn't help but think she looked like an angel with her creamy-white skin and small smooth lips. Although her hair was ebony black, he pictured it as a halo fanning out over her pillow and framing her face. She must be having a good dream because the smile was resonating on her slumbering face. When she stilled, Robert kissed her forehead. Then he bent down and whispered he loved her in her ear.

It took him a great deal of effort to tear himself away. She was so beautiful, caring, kind, and above all, an amazing person. In essence, she was a blessing. His heart ached deeply with the knowledge he would have to leave her. Even though it was God's plan, Robert deemed it unfair. As a man of faith, it was up to him to be strong and see it through. Hopefully he would be rewarded with a rather painless passing.

When he finally decided to get up, he figured it would be good to begin his typical morning routine. He went for a run, took a shower, brushed his teeth, and combed his hair. He even made himself breakfast. Alex was not out of bed yet, so he left her a plate on the kitchen counter with different breakfast foods. He then headed for the office. She didn't normally like breakfast, but he wanted to do something nice for her. It allowed him to feel a little less guilty over leaving without her today.

Robert considered riding to work together a benefit before now. Even though it had been only a week, he realized it was going to be nearly impossible from hereon out. His treatments began directly after work, and he needed to get back and forth without her knowledge. It was going to be a challenge to hide the bruising at his elbow. Being a human pincushion would certainly be noticeable even to the untrained eye. His wife noticed everything. It was a talent he knew made her such an asset in the advertising game.

As he headed in, he thought about ways to keep life as "normal" as possible and still get his treatment. Could he go during his lunch then come back without anyone missing him? He doubted that very seriously. This was not going to be easy at all.

❧

Alex rolled over and stretched to reach for the blaring alarm. She wiped the sleep from her tired eyes and looked around the room. It was then she noticed the empty space beside her. *That was odd*. Robert was always there with her in the morning. Her next thought caused her to shake her head. *Well, not so much lately.*

She swept her short legs out from under the covers and over the side of the mattress. She looked down and slipped her feet into a worn but fuzzy pink pair of slippers as she muffled a rather large yawn with her petite hand. She extended her arm to pick up her blue silk robe off the dressing table. Then she yelled for Robert, but he did not answer. She slipped the lush fabric over her shoulders and slid her arms inside the sleeves. She couldn't find the belt she regularly used to tie it up tight, so she folded it across her body and then wrapped her arms while tucking her hands underneath each one. She had to ward off the morning chill because she couldn't snuggle with Robert. She hated that he had come in late, and she hadn't even gotten to say good night. Then she couldn't say good morning.

She stumbled into the kitchen to begin brewing her morning cup of coffee. *It is going to need to be strong*, she thought to herself. Then she noticed the plate of food sitting on the counter. She smiled to herself. He *had* thought of her this morning. She wasn't up for food, but the thought really made her feel a little better. Then she noticed a note; it read,

> Dear Alex,
>
> I'm sorry I had to leave for work a little early. I'm not sure if I'll be able to help out on the job for Julius today until later. Go ahead and get started when you get there. I'll do my best to meet up with you in the conference room at 10am. The Mustang is in the garage. Feel free to take it today.
>
> Love,
> Robert

Alex looked at the clock and saw it was 8:00 a.m. He must have left early to do all of this. It was best if she got going to make it on time for work. She'd have to take her coffee with her this morning. No time to dawdle. At this rate, it was going to be a long day.

It was morning in the capital city, and Walter was heading to the office. The air was crisp and clean, something that he never had when he was in California. As part of his new morning routine, he was able to take a run through the heart of downtown. It was a time for him to reflect upon the direction his life was going.

Walter knew Julius needed help at the Columbus office. Although this task seemed difficult, he knew his team could raise more profits than the other MCD offices. Walter had been thinking of what plans needed to be put into place. The problem was he knew his quality of work had the possibility to be very affected. One word explained it all: *Alex*, he thought to himself.

When it came to it, Walter had to admit he was excited to see Alex more than he was getting involved in the day-to-day work. She had been on his mind all night, and it made him feel despicable down to the core. In fact, if Walter had a wife like Alex, there was no way he would approve of another man's roving eye sizing her up. He would put a stop to that real quick. Now he needed to set his attraction aside and get down to business. He owed it to himself to do better, and he owed it to his friend.

After taking a long cold shower, Walter decided to dress in his best gray Ralph Lauren suit and favorite black Berluti shoes. He felt masculine, powerful, and proud. As he pulled his brand-new silver Chevy Camaro out of the parking garage, he waved to the garage attendant. He quickly pulled out on to West Rich Street and headed right through the River South District. He looked around and realized he hadn't gotten an opportunity to take in the local scene. It was something he definitely needed to do. He could feel the heartbeat of the city as he drove by each historic building. *Soon*, he thought longingly.

The sun began to shine over the horizon. Walter relished the rays and held his head up high. As he slipped on his black Ray-Ban sunglasses, he smiled a rather large smile. He was able to see hope for the first time since arriving.

8

Alex hurried through the entrance of the MCD garage and tried to calm her wayward hair. Since it was a beautiful but crisp morning and Robert had left her the convertible, Alex had decided to ride with the top down while she could. She wished she had a brush. *She had everything else.* She laughed to herself.

This morning, the meteorologist on channel 6 had predicted an 80 percent chance of rain later today. Thank goodness Alex had brought along her umbrella. She also had her purse, briefcase, raincoat, coffee mug, and sweater for the chill that always settled in her office. When she pulled into her parking space, she realized it was certainly going to be a juggling act to get everything into the office. *Oh well*, she thought to herself.

She opened the car door and grabbed everything out of the backseat. Once she got everything in her hands and began walking, she realized she should have put the raincoat or sweater on. *It would have made life a lot easier.* She laughed.

Alex normally was more put together. She just needed to slow down and settle into the day. When it came down to it, she hated coming in by herself. She always felt so out of sorts when that happened.

Mixed Emotions

While walking with some quick steps, Alex looked down and threw her keys into her purse. Unfortunately, she didn't see the patch of oil on the ground or the opening elevator doors before her heels slipped out from under her.

❧

While waiting in the garage elevator as it took him to the correct office floor, Walter looked at his Blackberry and checked his e-mail. He was deep in thought when he heard the *ding* signaling the elevator was stopping to pick up another passenger. He moved to the right so he could make room for the new rider to hop on.

Unfortunately, he didn't anticipate the new rider to come sliding face-first into the elevator. When the doors actually opened, Alex burst through waving her arms and throwing everything at him in her hands—including the coffee. He caught her, and they both fell to the floor.

Once again he found himself doused with the caffeinated beverage and a flustered Alex in his arms. The doors tried to close, but Alex's feet were in the way. Walter noticed a broken heel and an oil spot right outside on the ground and realized this was what made Alex fall. "Alex," a soaked Walter uttered, "we really need to stop meeting like this."

Alex didn't hear anything Walter said. He rolled her over so her back was against his chest. Her eyes were closed, and her head was back. Walter wasn't sure if she had hurt herself or if she had passed out. He knew the collision had definitely knocked the wind out of him.

He shook her just a little and started to stand, balancing both of them at the same time. It certainly was difficult with an uncooperative partner. Suddenly, Alex let out a loud cry. It was a sound of utter despair. Walter was so startled he slammed back against the wall, and the doors shut once again. He sputtered, not knowing what in the goodness to do now.

⁂

Alex thought she heard Walter's voice as she felt herself come back into focus. Suddenly, she felt her body lift at the aid of someone else. Her ankle was throbbing, and she couldn't help but let out this guttural rather unorthodox sound as she began to rest her weight on it. Whoever it was must have been as startled as she was by the sound she made. She felt his body become stiff but continued to hold her up straight.

She couldn't remember where she was, and she certainly couldn't figure out why someone needed to help her. Her eyes opened, and she turned her head to see a soaking wet Walter and everything, including her coffee, on the ground. She thought, *No way! I cannot believe this happened again.* It was then Alex took in a deep breath and stared at Walter.

9

It was a beautiful spring-like day in Columbus, Ohio. The birds were chirping, and the sun was shining brightly down on the newly budding flowers and freshly cut green grass.

Kayla Taylor felt on top of the world as she walked around the Ohio State University campus. She loved the beginning of each semester because it gave her a chance to stand out in a sea of students. Usually, every professor dismissed her because she was blond, attractive, and conscious of her day-to-day fashion. They soon realized she had the brains to match. Kayla was smart, funny, and most importantly, vogue.

Kayla had lost track of time leading up to the start of this semester. She decided to call her mom, a routine she had grown accustomed to in her sophomore year of school. Since it was later in the afternoon, Alex should be available to talk. It had been at least a week since they last spoke, and Kayla knew indisputably she would hear about that once she connected with Alex.

As she came to the crosswalk, she saw a familiar car pull around the corner and head north. She could have sworn her dad was in that car, but he should be at the office with her mom, not on campus. It must have been her imagination, she thought.

She turned the corner and headed north, continuing toward the Ohio State University Medical Center. Kayla liked to volunteer at least a few times a week in the children's wing of the James Cancer Clinic. She felt good supporting children during a very difficult period. Thinking of her day ahead, Kayla realized she was still holding her cell phone when Alex's voice mail picked up, announcing she was unavailable to take the call. She decided not to leave a message and hung up.

Continuing on her course, Kayla came to the doors right outside the vestibule to the building. When she turned to the left to place her cell phone in her purse, she noticed the same car she had observed just a few minutes earlier now parked in the patients' parking lot. Just as Kayla had originally thought, it was definitely her dad and mom's car. She looked around but did not see either of them. She'd have to ask them when she got done with her shift.

Walking into the building, she passed several groups of medical students writing copious notes while listening intently to many doctors. It was obvious to her that it was a busy day in the hospital. Kayla knew her night would be long but fulfilling. She hoped she would be able to see Doc Richardson, her dad's longtime friend. He was always so nice to her, and he answered her numerous questions. She really loved being able to help him out too. Monday was his regular day to make evening rounds. He'd check in at the nursing station and then walk down to the vending machines. Kayla knew

Mixed Emotions

his afternoon Mountain Dew was a vice he couldn't do without. Maybe she would be able to see him before he started his rounds to see his patients.

Since it was about time to start her shift, Kayla headed to the volunteers' locker room. Moving quickly around and through the crowd of visitors, medical personnel, and ever-present custodial staff, Kayla made her way to the back of the building, keeping her head down and thinking of her daily hospital chores.

As she pushed open the locker-room door, she could have sworn she saw her dad out of the corner of her eye. She quickly turned her head around, but whoever it was had vanished. *This was shaping up to be an interesting night*, she thought. Maybe she didn't feel well and was hallucinating. Kayla hoped she wasn't coming down with an illness or something like that. She had too much going on to deal with that now.

❧

Robert ducked behind a pillar just in the nick of time. He had completely forgotten that Kayla was volunteering at the hospital this evening. If she found out he had been there on anything but business, she was going to ask questions. If she asked questions, she would want answers. If she got answers, she would tell her mother. He wasn't ready for that just yet. He wanted to have a plan set into motion first.

Robert knew he had to get to Dr. Richardson before he mentioned anything to Kayla. She was so fond of him, and he may not have realized Robert was not telling his family, at least not yet. He quickly took his cell phone from his pocket and dialed his longtime friend. He hoped he could reach him before Doc bumped into his daughter.

10

Doc Richardson sat in his office looking at the mound of folders and lab results of all the patients he had seen over the past two weeks. The sun was just beginning to crest over the smaller buildings, and his shift at the hospital had ended. His head was swimming with the numerous diagnoses he had given, and the number of dictations he still needed to do. Doc tried to forget about the number of patients he still needed to see upon his return to the office. He pulled the top folder off the pile and glanced at the label. Robert Taylor. Of course, the folder had to be one of the most important people to him, but most troubling too.

He closed the folder and returned it to the top of the mound. It had only been a couple of weeks since Robert had decided to go along with the experimental medicine because things weren't getting any easier. From a medical point of view, the treatments weren't going well, and Robert was stalling in telling his family. Sure, as a doctor, he had a Hippocratic oath to uphold, but this was one of those times where something had to be done. Maybe he just needed to do a little more convincing, so Robert took him more seriously.

Doc stood, stretched, and then pushed in his tall leather-backed office chair. He loosened his tie and turned off the light. As he dug his keys out of the right pocket of his lab coat, he hoped some type of resolution would come to him soon. He knew Robert was working on borrowed time right now.

For the time being, Doc decided he had to put more thought into it later. He needed to get home to his own wife; with all the loss in his life, he couldn't afford to lose her too.

❧

As a husband and father, Robert had spent most of his adult years providing for his family, supporting him, and helping Alex take care of the day's ins and outs. He remembered all the wiped noses, scraped knees, and held hands. Robert relished the times of struggle and triumph. All the things a good family man should do. *Right?* But how would his family respond to this unusual bout of selfishness? So what if he was sick? He didn't want them to know. It was his problem. Not theirs. Exasperated, he sighed. Then he put his head down and said, "Ugh… whom am I kidding?"

He was lying to himself. His family would support him, probably rearrange their lives for him. After all he had been through with the death of his mother and uncle, Robert swore he wouldn't make anyone bear the burden of making decisions for him when he couldn't any longer. It was like being judge and executioner or playing God. It wasn't a good place to be. In an instant, he thought of his life in pictures. Snapshots of the past came rushing to his mind. He settled into his own thoughts of life and love.

It hadn't been long into his marriage before their two children were born. Their daughter, Kayla, had her mother's face but his eyes. Incredibly, she had a striking shade of golden-blond hair that neither of them could understand. It was one of her traits that set her apart just like her mother's eyes always did. Robert always felt she was a beautiful mix of them both.

At twenty, she was relatively set in her life's path. She had aspired to become a doctor ever since she was a little girl. It seemed as though she had always been able to handle the weight of the world with seemingly little to no cares. To be honest, the more he thought about it, she may have enough backbone and strength to support him in the toughest moments. Maybe she could help him see this all the way through. *Then again*, Robert thought, *could she?*

In fact, if Robert were inclined to tell anyone, it would be his son. The problem was, Preston was just nineteen. Although considered grown in the eyes of the law, he wasn't sure his son could bear the responsibility of knowing this type of secret. He never had been good at keeping things from his mother. You would think, with as close of a relationship they shared, he'd look like her little twin; but actually, he was the spitting image of Robert all the way down to his pinky toes. Interestingly enough, Alex always thought he was more reflective than Robert. "More like an old soul," she once said.

One thing was for sure, no matter what the problem was, Preston would weigh all the options, see whom it would affect, and then think about it some more. This wasn't to say that Robert didn't consider these things; he just separated business and pleasure. Business was business. Robert's motto was "Never make a bed where you keep your business." When asked about Alex, he liked to say, "You always have to make at least one exception to your own rules."

In the end, if solely based upon family dynamics, Robert knew Preston would step up and see to it that everyone's needs were met. Then again, he couldn't help but think about his daughter's systematic approach and need to finish a project no matter the difficulty or feelings involved. Robert knew it was nearing time to say something. The only question left was, should he tell him?

༄

Looking out the windshield and much to his surprise, Robert noticed the sign indicating he had reached MCD, LLC. The car seemed to have steered itself toward the office. Robert shook his head. He couldn't figure out how he had managed to get there in one piece. He really hadn't been paying the least bit of attention to the road, let alone the task of driving. He realized now he had been taking for granted all these daily activities he'd grown so accustomed to doing. The simplest and most mundane tasks all seemed to hold a different type of importance or significance now. He probably should be thinking more of these things too.

As Robert exited the car and headed for the parking-garage elevator, he thought more and more about the choice he had made to keep his family unaware of his illness. He couldn't even say the word *cancer*. It disgusted him to even utter it!

He was stressed and tired. He knew he wouldn't be able to keep this charade going for much longer. He felt Alex's quizzical eyes continuously study him day in and day out.

He had to make up more and more excuses about leaving early or traveling separately from her. The work that he did with both her and Walter was taking its toll on him. Either that or the treatments were not working as well as projected.

It was time to have a serious heart-to-heart with Doc about the status of his treatment. If the prognosis was accurate and he only had about a month and a half left, he had to do something fast. *How did the saying go?* "Drastic time calls for drastic measures."

11

The weeks were going by very fast, and Alex noticed her husband was getting more and more reclusive. Although he was working on the same project, he was hardly around. Unfortunately, she hadn't seen him this morning as she had hoped either. She wanted to know what was going on. Why wouldn't he spend more than an hour with her here and there? She had to get to the bottom of this. She had to do it, or she was going to lose it!

She walked the hallways all over the office but still no Robert. This was annoying. Truly it was pissing her off. *Well, no more Mrs. Nice Girl*, she thought. Being the queen of the social network or the proverbial grapevine so to speak, Tamara had to know something. Alex decided to march herself over to her friend. If anyone knew anything, it would be her.

As she walked down the hallway, Alex noticed the fluorescent light was shining down on to the top of Tamara's blond-tipped hair. She was glad her friend was sitting at her desk. Alex smiled looking at how Tamara's round face was looking down at a file, and her button nose was scrunched up and wrinkled. *Trying to look busy*, Alex inferred. Her chin was sectioned with a little line down

Mixed Emotions

the middle, and her hand was propped underneath. As Alex came closer, Tamara looked up. "Whatcha doing, girl?" she said with a smile. Alex leaned forward over the top of the desk and signaled for Tamara to move closer to her. Tamara obliged.

"I need your help." Alex was serious.

Tamara was puzzled, and an oh-this-should-be-good look spread across her face. She asked Alex, "Why?"

Alex stilled her trembling hands. She was quite resolved as she shared her heart with her friend. "I'm worried about Robert. He's gone at all hours. He doesn't spend more than an hour or two with me. And I have no idea when the last time was he talked with the kids." Alex's eyes began to hold deep pockets of tears. She didn't think she could keep them from spilling over.

Tamara was floored by this news, but she wanted to assure her friend that she could support her. "Sweetie, I have no idea, but if he's up to no good, I'll find out." Alex was relieved. Then Tamara said what Alex had been wondering deep down. "Could he be having an affair?"

Alex just didn't want to think her husband could do something that low, but as her friend patted her on the shoulder, she placed her face in her hands. She pleaded without even lifting her head, "Tamara, just do what you need to. I've just got to know." Her voice trailed off as she said, "If I find out he is…"

Alex lifted her head and looked into the eyes of her friend. She didn't need to say anything else. She knew Tamara was on the case. Now it was time to head toward her work session with Walter. A stop at the restroom was probably in order. Hopefully she didn't look a fright.

She didn't want to embarrass herself any more than she had a couple weeks ago with her new colleague.

In order to get her thoughts straight, Alex headed for the restroom to freshen up. Then she headed to the coffeepot for a fresh cup of joe. Finally, she walked to the conference-room door, pausing for a moment to think about what to do next. She looked down at the carpet and closed her eyes.

"It can't be all that bad to see me."

Alex knew that voice, a baritone that came to her like a quiet whisper, causing chills to go down her spine. Startled by her own body's reaction, Alex opened her eyes and turned her head to find Walter leaning in close. He smelled of fresh woods and pure man. He smiled at her then pushed his arm out to hold open the office door.

Alex laughed a nervous laugh but felt rattled down to the core. She said, "Well…," but when she looked in his eyes, she lost what she was going to say. It had to be the time away from her husband. She would never respond this way to a man outside her marriage. *Would she?*

She shook her head and set her resolve to head to the conference table. Unfortunately, it wasn't but a second into the room that she stopped staring straight ahead, causing Walter to run smack-dab into her back.

❧

Walter was right behind Alex as she stopped dead in her tracks. He couldn't seem to fathom what made her stop so abruptly. Then he looked over her shoulder and saw Robert, or the back of him, facing toward their boss. This made Walter rather curious. The grapevine was running rampant through the office. Alex had been on the warpath this morning looking for said husband. He hated listening to gossip, but when it came to Alex, Walter couldn't help it. He was that wrapped up into her.

For the life of him, Walter couldn't figure out why she didn't know where he was all morning. What had been so difficult? He was standing right there in front of her! It was then Walter noticed a change in Alex's demeanor. Her body language had altered from solemn to pure agitation. Obviously, her speculated anger from before had some solid foundation. She was beginning to unravel right here in front of them all.

Walter realized at that moment that it was more than anger. He had a sneaking suspicion that she had no idea Julius was going to be at this meeting. For Walter, he had to admit he was rather relieved too. He hadn't been expecting Julius either.

☙❧

Seriously? Here, she had been looking all over damnation for her husband, and he was standing right here in front of her. She was so pissed! Then on top of that her boss had been there too?

Of course, no one had notified her of this development while she had been playing private eye around the office. She thought her friend had the lowdown on everything. Obviously, Tamara wasn't as good at getting all the details as Alex had thought. It seemed like they were interrupting a private meeting between her boss and husband. Maybe instead of being mad at the fact she didn't know what was going on, she should focus on the interaction right before her.

Was Julius waiting to hear Robert say something? Or had it been the other way around? Maybe Robert had been waiting to tell him something and had been interrupted. A thought that was confirmed when Robert shifted his eyes to look at her and she saw the ache resonating from them. She had been noticing that look more and more lately. God, how she wished she could help him through whatever was happening. Even if it was something that could make her say, mad. She had made a vow a long time ago to stay through sickness and through health, through richer and through poorer, and was bound to stand behind it.

12

"What type of man thinks about a married woman not his own?" Walter chastised himself. He had to get over whatever it was that was attracting him to Alex. The way she looked. The way she smelled. It just had to be the loneliness caused by the loss of his love and the move. When he saw her standing there outside the conference-room door, she looked crushed. He just wanted to reach out to make sure she was OK. But was he overstepping his bounds? Again he relied on humor. That seemed to be the best angle in this situation.

The past two weeks had been comfortable working side by side with Alex. Her husband wasn't as involved. He knew Alex had completed most of the groundwork. Walter originally thought he would be. Sure Alex had different reasons for Robert's numerous absences, but Walter truly hadn't minded. They had laughed over the ridiculous ideas both of them had pitched to get new clients on board. They even had come up with some viable ideas too.

He had learned a great deal about her in such a short period of time. Everything was great. Well, except the fact she had a husband. That was—unfortunate. Today was going to be different.

Walter could tell that the minute he entered the conference room and saw the way Alex looked at Robert, there was a pain there. Possibly, even a little anger. *This should be interesting*, Walter thought to himself.

༄

Julius had been available for a brief minute, and Robert thought it was a perfect moment to talk about his situation. He didn't want to call it an illness. Thinking of it as a problem that needed a solution was much easier than facing the truth. Unfortunately, it was getting harder and harder to deny. He knew this illness was more than even Doc originally thought. He had finally come to terms with the reality. It really wasn't if he passed from this disease but more like when he passed. Whenever it was, he wanted to have all his affairs in order. He didn't want his family to have any worries.

The young CEO was sitting in the conference room scrolling through something on his iPad. Robert hated to interrupt, but he knew his time alone was limited. "Uh, Julius, may I speak with you please?" He walked over and sat down to the left of his boss.

He looked up and responded to Robert's request. "Of course. What can I do for you?" He said with a smile. "I was just looking over the work your team has been doing. Good stuff."

Robert was flattered, but he couldn't take the credit. With his treatments, he was barely around. "To be

Mixed Emotions

honest, I can't take all of the credit for the work. In fact, that's what I wanted to talk with you about."

Julius looked rather perplexed. He wasn't sure what his employee meant. "What do you mean? I specifically told the three of you that you were to be working as a team. Did I not make myself *clear*?" *Great*, Robert thought, *he put great emphasis on the last word.*

Robert took a deep breath. *Well, better get this over with*, he thought. Looking square into his superior's eyes, he wanted to speak as clearly as he possible. The emotion behind this topic began to ache in his heart and choked him a little. Just as he began to explain his condition, the door to the conference room opened once again, and Robert's opportunity slipped right out of his hands.

He wished that he had just a few more moments alone with Julius before Walter and Alex had come into the room. He turned around and looked at Alex. He hurt inside when he looked at her. Then he looked just past her to his new colleague and something he hadn't noticed before hit him right in the face. Was that *interest* he saw in the other man's eyes? Something deep inside Robert started to take hold of him. He couldn't tell if it was jealousy, anger, or something else altogether?

"Robert," Alex spoke almost in a whisper. He didn't respond. She could see that he was in some sort of daydream. *Ugh! What is going on with him?*

She walked up to him and lightly touched his arm. Robert shook his head and smiled up at her. He placed his hand on top of hers. "Robert, may I speak to you for a minute?" Alex nodded her head to the right to indicate she meant outside the conference room. He nodded his head yes. She turned to her colleague and said, "Walter, we'll be right back. Could you please update Mr. Whinehart on the project?"

❧

Walter looked at Julius and then again to her. "Sure," he responded.

He seemed a little caught off guard, but Alex didn't have time to worry about him too. She could hear Walter begin pitching the concept ideas to Julius as she headed out the door. Robert followed closely behind her.

The minute they were out of earshot, Alex rounded on Robert. "WHAT IS WRONG WITH YOU AND WHERE IN THE SAM HECK HAVE YOU BEEN?" She couldn't seem to suppress her feelings.

Robert's eyes grew to the size of silver dollars. He started to stutter. "What…what…what do you mean?"

Truly? Did he really not understand? Sometimes he could be so dense. "Robert, I just don't get what is happening to you. You look ill. You disappear for hours at a time. I want to spend time with you, and you…you just…you just aren't around." Suddenly, a tear started to fall down her cheek. She hated showing such emotion at work, but she couldn't hold back anymore.

Robert was speechless. In his heart, he hated seeing Alex so upset. He moved closer and cupped her face in his hands. "Alex, honey, you are my world. Your smile melts my heart. I've never loved anyone as much as I do you and this family."

Alex was looking right into his eyes. He didn't want to lie to her, so he decided to tell her just a little bit more than he had considered doing before now. "I haven't felt well, but don't worry, I went and saw Doc. He said I must have had a virus, and he gave me a couple of medications to take. I'm sorry that you have been worried."

He wasn't sure Alex was going to be satisfied with his explanation. She was not easy to fool, nor would it be easy to appease her curiosity. Alex pulled back from Robert and crossed her arms across her chest. *Crap*, he thought to himself. *This isn't good*. He readied himself for whatever she had to say.

"What about the unanswered calls, late nights, and the disappearing in the early mornings? Then you are leaving work without me…" She probed further. Her voice was starting to rise, and she started to point her finger. "You expect me to believe that…that…nonsense?"

Bless her heart. Even when she was mad, she couldn't bring herself to curse. Robert smiled, and Alex's eyebrows went up in a don't-mess-with-me kind of way. He backed up and tried to focus. Then Robert felt the eyes of their coworkers starting to gawk their way. He decided to usher Alex to her office where their domestic dispute couldn't be a spectacle for all to see. Of course, her meddlesome assistant was straining to hear what was going on. It was all Robert could do not to say something to him. What was his name again? Truly it didn't matter.

The little weasel, Robert thought. *He needs to get busy with something other than prying in other people's business.* Robert decided to give him a curt nod and walked right past, closing the door once he and Alex were through. *There!* Now he felt better.

Alex stood stone straight. Her face was beginning to turn a dark shade of red. Robert was surprised; his wife's anger came so fast these days. *Man, she's really mad*, he thought to himself.

He decided it was time for a little embellishment, so to speak, something to talk her down off the ledge of insanity. "Honey, don't be mad. I promise there is nothing odd going on. I've just been working out a little bit more. Keeping my stress down like Doc suggested."

She cocked her head to the side in a disgusted manner. She lifted one eyebrow and said, "Robert, I love you. We have been through many ups and downs over the years, but so help me God if you are up to no good, I will make life *very* bad for you."

With that, she breezed right past him and flung open the door. It hit the outer office wall and sounded a loud bang. Everyone turned to stare, a disbelieving Robert standing there in utter disbelief.

Robert shook his head and closed the door again. He needed to sit down. He looked all around and decided to take refuge behind his wife's desk. He turned around in her swivel chair and pulled the picture of his children and wife off the credenza. He rubbed his finger down the beach-themed frame. He remembered Alex had purchased it as a vacation souvenir. The picture showed his family all dressed in white and sitting on top of a sand dune. The water was stunningly blue, and the sun was setting with a ray of colors casting throughout the sky and reflecting a pink hue off the water.

He remembered that trip to North Carolina with fondness, a favorite location for his family to travel. He felt blessed to have taken this particular picture of his family. Usually Alex would have been taking pictures, but he convinced her it was a moment he wanted to capture forever. He touched the glass above the faces of his children then turned his attention to the image of Alex. He thought about the questions she had today. He just couldn't think of any good answers for her now.

Robert felt the vibrations of his cell phone in the front pocket of his jacket. He reached in and pulled it out. Then he looked at the caller ID. Doc was calling. *This cannot be good.* "Robert Taylor," he said as he answered the phone.

Doc's pleasant voice said, "Robert. It's Doc. We need to talk."

Robert could feel the urgency in his voice. "Sure, Doc. What do you need?"

ೊ

Doc felt a rush of fear and sadness all in one breath when Robert answered the phone. He hated having to tell him such poor news. He said, "Your treatment is not helping to reduce the amount of infected cells in your system. The cancer is the same strength and not responding to the treatment. I am trying to determine what to do next, but I haven't given up."

Robert's thoughts drifted to his treatments with Doc and the length at which he had to go to keep everything a secret. "Doc, I can't hold on much longer. It all feels like a dog-and-pony show. I'm worn out and can't take much more."

"Look, Robert, I'm going to get in contact with another colleague. It will take me a day though, so try to stay positive." With that, Doc hung up the phone.

"Hello? Doc?" All Robert heard was the dial tone. He just couldn't think of what to do. Suddenly, Robert remembered he had a plan. It was time to make things happen. As his decision began to take hold, all the feelings deep down inside him started to ease. It was time to seek reinforcements.

※

Alex managed to gather herself and head back to the conference room. She was so angry. She really did not want to work, but if she didn't, she was probably going to kill her husband. As she rounded the corner to go back into the conference room, she saw Walter standing just outside the door. He seemed to hesitate at first, but then he flashed that amazing smile. Alex's heart skipped a beat, and she felt butterflies in her stomach. "Oh, this can't be good," Alex said to herself.

She walked up to Walter and said, "Are you finished already? I thought he would have a million questions." There was no way they got off that easy. Julius always had more to add or tweak. He'd never be happy without his additional input. Then he might be satisfied enough to put his stamp of approval on it.

"Not exactly," Walter relayed.

Curious, Alex lifted her eyebrow. She said, "I thought so." It wasn't really a surprise. Alex knew something else would have to be done. Julius had never approved anything on the first go-around.

"He really wasn't thrilled that Robert hasn't been a part of the process," Walter said.

"Well, join the rest of us!" Alex's thought came out before she even realized it. She covered her mouth and said, "I'm sorry, Robert, I mean, Walter. This hasn't been the best couple of weeks."

Alex noticed Walter look toward the ground. *Was he upset?* Did she say something wrong? That was when she realized he must have thought she included him in the "rough last couple of weeks" comment. "Well, except for the time with you," she added almost in a whisper.

❧

This time, it was Walter's eyebrows that shot up. *Interesting,* he thought. *She just might like spending time with me. I knew it!* He smiled, and mentally high-fived himself. *I still have it.* Then he said to her, "Look, I haven't been able to unpack the boxes in my office, so we wouldn't be comfortable in there. Let's go into your office and talk further." He motioned for Alex to join him. As she passed, he took in her scent of Japanese cherry blossom and Dove soap. A scent he had grown to love over the past couple of weeks. A smell he realized he never wanted to do without again.

At first he thought the afternoon was going to be terrible. Julius had nothing but disdain for the ideas the team, well, Walter, had presented. Of course it had to be *him* that got the earful. Julius didn't hold back even when it came to his old friend. Now as Walter sat staring at Alex and discussing what to do next, the afternoon was shaping up quite nicely after all.

13

Preston Taylor had a sneaking suspicion that his father was not OK. Either that or he was trying to guilt him into doing something, most probably for his mother. Robert's rambling message had made no sense. *It was almost incoherent*, Preston thought.

As he ran his hand through his shaggy dark-brown hair, Preston reflected more about the voice mail his father had left about an hour ago. Honestly, he didn't feel like calling his dad back right now. The problem was Preston's subconscious just wouldn't let him off that easy.

"Great, what do I do now?" he said to no one in particular. Preston decided then to pull his smartphone out and call his dad back. Maybe he'd be able to ease in and out of a conversation, but then again, who was he kidding?

Preston quickly dialed his father's number. As he waited, the phone just rang and rang until finally on the eighth ring, Robert answered. "Son, I'm so glad you called. I need your help."

Great, I knew it, Preston thought. "Dad, I'm really busy. I don't think I have enough time to be of any help," he said as convincingly as he could. Unfortunately, Robert wasn't listening. He forged right on ahead with what he had to say. All Preston could do was just shake his head. He had learned a long time ago not to interrupt his parents.

"Listen. There is a new guy in the office. Name's Walter Messenger. I think he's a big fraud. He seems to have Julius eating out of the palm of his hand. I want you to call your friend. What's his name...Matthews? You know the one that's a private investigator."

What in the name of all that's holy? Preston couldn't help but think as he responded to Robert. "Dad, you mean Ben Matthews?" He didn't know what in the world had gotten into his father. "Dad, I don't get it," he persisted. "Since when do you worry about the people at your workplace?"

He thought he didn't want to get involved before he called his dad back, and now he knew why! He most certainly didn't want to now. "Dad, I don't know. Ben may not be able to help you out. What is this about?"

Robert started to explain further, "Julius has us working with a new guy. As I told you before, his name is Walter Messenger. He came out of the Sacramento office. He's been working a lot with your mother, and I want to make sure he isn't some two-bit hustler. You never know, son, he could be some escaped *criminal.*"

He knew his dad had put the emphasis on the last word on purpose. Robert knew Preston just couldn't, more like wouldn't, say no to remain cautious for his mother's safety.

Preston's eyebrows scrunched together. Then he brought his right hand up to press the fingertips to the bridge of his nose. He took a deep breath and decided he'd humor his father, but not before asking him one last question. "Dad, have you talked with mom about this?" He hated to question his dad's judgment, but he did seem a little, uh, *crazed*.

Robert's tone became almost pleading. "No, son. I don't want to involve your mom in this, at least for now. OK?"

Preston grimaced. *Oh man, not letting mom in on this was bad news.* Preston knew, however, he really couldn't upset his dad either. *Mom would get over it before dad would. Hopefully...*

"All right, Dad, I'll see what Ben can do." He hung up after receiving his dad's repeated thanks. *Weird*, he thought again to himself. Before he called his friend Ben, he needed some time to think.

Great! Robert thought to himself. The first part of his plan was in place. He had his son convinced he needed his help. Ben Matthews was going to do some investigation, and no one else would be none the wiser.

Robert's gut said nothing would come of the investigation, but he wanted to make sure he was accurate. He thought his make-believe reasons appeased Preston. He certainly hoped they were good enough. Now he needed to put step two into action. Time was running short for him, and he knew this next project may be more difficult. If fact he *planned* on it!

క్రిం

Walter sat facing his fireplace, sipping on a glass of bourbon he truly didn't want to drink. The sun on the Columbus skyline had already set once again. He thought, *Another day gone down the drain. This is not what I wanted at all.* Then again, he did get to spend the afternoon looking into Alex's green eyes. Maybe that's why he suddenly felt restless; those eyes haunted him even in his sleep.

He glanced around the room and noticed all of the boxes still sitting in the same spots they had been for over a month. He stood and walked over to a stack waiting to be unpacked. He pulled open a flap on the top box and then the other side flap too. As he went to put his hand inside and pull out the contents, the doorbell rang. He had no idea who would be calling this late at night. *Might be the neighbor,* he thought. He did see her peeking out of her door earlier. He always felt her watching, or more like spying, when he came in at night. *Hopefully not,* he thought. *I'm certainly not in the mood to be hospitable.*

Walking toward the door, he heard a persistent knock. "Coming," he announced before he reached for the handle. He looked into the peephole to see who had knocked. He liked to be prepared for anything. When he looked, however, he never expected what, or rather who, was looking back at him.

14

Robert wasn't sure, but he thought he heard someone moving behind the door though no one had yet answered. He decided to knock loudly, just in case Walter hadn't heard the ring. He never thought in a million years he'd have to be standing at a stranger's door, asking one of the hardest questions of his life. He looked at his watch and noticed it was ten o'clock at night.

He hated calling upon someone so late, but he realized after his news from Doc that there was no time to delay. Although he felt terrible and really just wanted to go home to cuddle with his wife, Robert knew putting his plan into action would be now or never. *Hopefully, Walter will be receptive to this proposition,* he thought.

There would be a lot of questions, and Robert wasn't sure he'd have all the answers right now. Alex would have another round of questioning for him when he got home too. Not being home was taking its toll on both of them. *I better get used to it,* he reminded himself. He'd be challenging himself soon enough.

Robert heard a muffled voice then the doorknob rattle. As the door started to open, Walter peeked around the door with a puzzled look upon his face. Robert couldn't blame him. It was rather odd for him to come, let alone come unannounced.

Walter cleared his throat. "Uh, Mr. Taylor, I wasn't expecting anyone, much less you." But he gave Robert an easy smile and extended his hand. Robert shook it firmly. "Is everything OK? I hate to say it, but you really don't look… well."

Walter had hit the nail on the head and hadn't even heard what Robert had to say. *Very perceptive,* he thought. He looked at Walter and said, "That's why I'm here, Walter. I have something I need to discuss with you. May I come in?"

Obviously, Walter was caught off guard, but he moved to the side and welcomed Robert into his home. "Sure, come on in." Walter signaled, and Robert walked past him. While he followed, he apologized for the state of his house. "I'm sorry I haven't had much time to unpack, but please make yourself comfortable. Would you like a drink?"

Robert would have loved a drink, but he needed to get straight to the point. The burden of this illness was weighing heavily on his chest. He had to get started, or he may never get what he had to say out. "No, thank you. I won't be here long."

Walter's spacious loft had an incredible view of the city and obviously came with a high price tag. Robert couldn't help but notice the amazing details put into the living space. *He appreciates the finer things,* he thought. Finally, he made his way over to the fireplace and began to stare at the incandescence.

Walter joined Robert at the fireplace. He asked, "What can I do you for?"

Robert was taken aback by his question. It was something Alex always said to him. The little play on words drove Robert crazy when they first married, but as time went on, it was something he thought was rather charming about her.

He turned away from Walter and went to a sleek-looking black couch. Robert lowered himself onto the couch and stretched his legs. Then he crossed them at his ankles and reclined his back, settling into the large cushions. *Definitely designer*, he figured. His fingers slid over the top of the cushion next to him. *Good, the man has taste*, he concluded.

"Well, let me get right to the point." Robert adjusted so he could look more directly at Walter. He noticed a change in Walter's positioning as his interest piqued. Then he watched as Walter came to sit in front of him.

"I've noticed in the short time we have been working together, you're rather perceptive. In fact, you were right on point with your deduction when I arrived."

Curious, Walter leaned forward, so his elbows reposed on his knees. Then he rested the weight of his head on his palms. His eyes, however, looked directly at Robert without wavering. Sensing Walter was ready for whatever he had to say, Robert continued, "I've been told I have stage four pancreatic cancer. My treatment began the week you moved here, but the successes have been slow. My doctor feels it's time for me to consider other… options."

Walter knew something serious had been going on, he could just sense it. What he couldn't figure out though, was how he could help in this situation. He barely knew the man who sat before him. He went to say as much, but Robert interrupted his chain of thought.

"You see, Walter, I know it's not *if* I die…but actually *when*…" he paused in his thought. When Robert went to speak to him once again, he now faced Walter as the businessman he had always been known to be.

Robert smiled. "I'm here to discuss a contract of sorts, one involving my wife…and you."

The thought of being with Alex uninterrupted and without complications was like a dream come true, but Walter knew in his heart, it would never be that easy. She was married to this man sitting in front of him. Her heart belonged to him. They had children, grown children. She would never be his to behold.

He sat back onto the cushion and turned so he could pick up his tumbler sitting on the glass coffee table next to him. He had considered taking a drink but, with the shock of hearing Robert's statement, paused in midair, never letting the glass reach his lips. He turned his head slightly to the side rather taken aback. He sat the glass back down and cleared his throat. Before he made any snap judgments or decisions, he'd have to hear Robert out.

"I'm sorry. I must have heard you incorrectly. Did you say *me* and your *wife?*" Instead of being able to say any more, Walter was rather short. The stoic look on Robert's face confirmed Walter had heard him correctly.

Robert must have instantly recognized a change in Walter's easygoing demeanor because he moved just a little. Walter had to admit his curiosity was obviously peaked, but a tinge of protectiveness had come over him too.

Good, Robert thought to himself. *He does care for Alex. I hope this works to my advantage.* He began giving Walter the details. "At this time, my family knows nothing about my illness. In fact, as I stated before, I had just received the news when you joined our team. I have been going to OSU Medical Center, but it's getting more and more difficult to hide the negative effects the treatments are inflicting."

☙❧

Walter nodded. He finally understood Alex's need to make excuses for her husband and the reason why Robert didn't join them more often during work sessions. Alex didn't know the truth behind it all.

To be honest, Walter rather liked the fact that he worked so closely with Alex. But he had to admit, it drove his passions to an utter uproar. She was incredible, and Robert should consider himself lucky. He'd been jealous of Robert all this time and felt annoyed about how he seemed to dismiss her so quickly. Now that Walter had learned the fate that lay ahead for each of them, he felt like an ass. Here her husband was sick, and he was obsessing over her. *Nice,* he thought to himself. He moved from his rather leisurely sitting position to place his elbows on his knees and lean his head on his closed fists. Robert seemed to be preparing to say something big, and Walter was still pretty intrigued.

With a slight cough, Robert continued his speech. "This past month, my actions have been rather out of character. You, my dear sir, have not seen me at my best. Normally my wife and I work together as one of the most formidable advertising teams in the country. Because of my illness and subsequent treatments, this has been completely dissolved. Alex is very perceptive, and she is definitely sensing something is wrong. My time to keep her at bay is dwindling. In my heart, I know it would hurt her too much to know the impending truth. I can't do that to her or our kids. To keep this from happening, I'm going to disappear. After careful consideration, I have chosen you to step in and take my place."

Walter was shocked. *I can't believe this is what he wanted to tell me. Really?* He shook his head in disagreement. Robert's proposal was preposterous. Walter was adamant. *I'm not getting involved.*

He knew this was not how the situation should be handled, especially after losing a loved one. He hadn't any prior knowledge nor the ability to prepare for her death. He would never have wished something like this to happen, even on his worst enemy. He was fond of Alex, rather too fond. He could not do this to her. As he spoke, he felt it his duty to convey how terrible of an idea this was for Robert to pursue.

"Look, Robert, I don't know what gave you the idea this would be a good solution to your problem, nor do I understand why you chose me to participate in this, this scheme." The hurt he felt after Shannon died came through in the words he spoke now to Robert. "I do not feel like participating in this charade, and I strongly suggest you go back to the drawing board and figure something else out." Walter hoped he got his point across, but Robert didn't even seem to shy away.

In some regard, Robert seemed to become more resolved in his decision. He stated, "Walter, this is the only idea that will work. I'm going to disappear. I need more treatment and have to leave soon. I have put into place all that you need. You will have full access to a lucrative portfolio of investments and a rather hardy sum in savings. You will use this money to see to it that my wife and kids are taken care of at all times. There is to be no mention of our arrangement or of my illness."

Walter went to interject something, but Robert didn't give him a chance. He asserted, "Don't tell me the idea of being with my wife doesn't interest you. I've seen the attraction you have for her. It's been written all over your face since the first time I met you in her office."

Oh man! Walter hoped he had hidden it. Robert knew about his allure for Alex. Now he had to convince him it wasn't a crush he was harboring for her. Maybe he could portray it as more of an admiration. He implored, "Robert, I would never dream of being with another man's wife, let alone interfere in a working relationship with two people. Of course, I think Alex is attractive, funny, caring, and kind, but..." He stopped there as Robert smiled a knowing smile. Walter started shaking his head. He thought, *Great. I guess I'll have to convince myself first.*

Robert stood and buttoned his suit jacket. He said, "Walter, I too was attracted to Alex the minute I laid eyes on her. I still am today. She is enchanting, to say the least, and she deserves the best. I have given her every part of me, and I'm trying to make this life change as easy as possible. She has always been the family rock. I would prefer her have anger for me rather than be heartbroken over my death any day."

Then he began heading toward the front door. Before he opened it, he turned to say one last thing. "I have little, if any, time left. You need to come to terms with the fact that this would be the right thing to do. Think this over so we can move forward. I will touch base with you tomorrow at noon. We'll meet for lunch at Schmidt's Sausage Haus in German Village. Please remember, say nothing to my wife or anyone else."

With that, he was gone. A dumbfounded Walter sat looking at the closed door.

Alex settled into bed with her beautiful black hair still wet from a dip in her nightly bath. She felt the luxurious Egyptian cotton sheets and fluffy down comforter Robert had insisted on buying her. Under her hands, she smoothed each piece to tuck herself in. Her creamy-white skin was soft from the lavender soak, and her mood was rather relaxed considering she was alone—*again*.

Robert was nowhere to be found, and she had given up trying to figure out what was going on. Everyone else was close-lipped. Whatever it was, she had to believe it was for the best. She had never known her husband to do anything purposefully to hurt her. Then she thought, *Why would she believe any different now?* Slowly her eyes started to close, and she fell into a deep sleep. Her worries started to slip away as a dream replayed a memory from not too long ago.

15

The sun was just peaking up over the horizon as Alex walked out of the hotel room onto the balcony overlooking the ocean of East Bali. It was the morning of her twentieth wedding anniversary, and she was still shocked that her husband had chartered a plane to this beautiful Indonesian island.

Today she was going to experience the exotic lure of what the locals called "the isle of the gods." Robert had promised to immerse her in a rainforest safari and later an aphrodisiac spa treatment. She had hoped with some convincing that she could get him to understand her need to bask in the tropical sunsets and swim in the pools that collected below high waterfalls. She slid quietly back into the room and smiled as she saw Robert lying there so peacefully. It was time to wake him to start their adventure together.

Although reluctant to get dressed in her bathing suit, she grabbed the one-piece she always felt most comfortable in. Like many women, she wanted to lose a few pounds, but Robert begged her not to get too skinny. She smiled at the way he chose to dismiss her self-conscious thoughts. He'd always say, "I like meat on your bones."

She could never figure out why he loved that she wasn't a Barbie-doll shape. She slipped the thick black straps on to her left then right shoulders. As she raised her head to look into the mirror, she realized Robert had been watching her the whole time, his passion emanating through his piercing blue eyes. Maybe she wouldn't have to do as much convincing as she thought. It seemed that if Robert had it his way, they just might not be going anywhere today or any of the other days of their trip.

Alex's dream continued to the days they spent soaking up the sun and drinking piña coladas. There was not enough energy for her or Robert to do much of anything else. Both of them had to rest to re-energize from the nights of lovemaking. She hated the thought of leaving that enchanted island and returning home.

She begged Robert to stay a little longer, but he told her to think of the responsibilities neither of them would think of not fulfilling. Even in her dream, Alex could still feel how it was this impending return to stateside that appeared to dull the excitement once again. She remembered how as they started to ascend on the plane ride home, she had closed her eyes and rested her head on the back of the airplane seat. Seemingly just minutes later, Alex had felt a nudge on her arm as Robert began to call her name.

When she finally opened her eyes, she realized she was at home. It was then that she realized her husband sat looking at her. He was already dressed and ready for work. She had been dreaming. She sighed as she thought, *If only I could go back to that time again.*

Once again, Alex looked peaceful as she slept. "If only I could tell her the truth," Robert whispered to himself. He was dreading the conversation this morning, but he couldn't slip out on her again. As he reached over to nudge her lightly, she rolled so the sun illuminated her face. He couldn't believe he had been so lucky to have her in his life. It made his resolve that much stronger. He whispered, "Sweetie, I need to go. Doc wanted to follow up with me, but I wanted to say I love you first."

Alex's green gaze fell upon Robert with stoic resolve. "I love you too, Robert."

Robert felt her love and knew it was now or never. He leaned down and kissed her forehead. He wanted to settle her, or really himself, by saying, "I'll see you at work."

Doc had negotiated with the Cleveland Clinic to have Robert come there and finish out the remaining doses. He was growing too weak and needed more distance to receive his treatment. He hoped his meeting with Walter went as planned. He didn't have room for any bumps in the road. Tomorrow was the day he left.

16

The computer screen flashed images of a confident-looking blond man in his late thirties standing in a designer suit. The photo showed his arm around a buxom redhead, and he seemed to have captivated the attention of everyone in the room. Walter Messenger was his name, and as a private investigator, Benjamin Matthews had been looking at his image for hours.

Recently, his friend from the Federal Bureau of Investigation had become engaged to his sister. He owed Ben a favor for keeping his mouth shut after a rather rambunctious bachelor party. In this field of work, Ben knew that his contacts were as valuable as the information he received from them. He took his job seriously.

Although strikingly handsome and styled just right, Ben had to make sure no one at the Panera Bread was watching too closely. Unfortunately, he was too good-looking for the other college coeds not to notice. Every now and again, he'd look over his shoulder, flipping his curly mocha locks, which seemed to signal one of the many beautiful girls sitting close to come his way. He'd flash his long eyelashes and chocolate eyes their way while politely declining. Obviously, he wasn't doing well. It took a couple dismissals before he was actually left alone.

To keep up with the act, he made sure to have a steaming cup of coffee at all times. He spread a notebook and laptop along the booth space he had acquired earlier this morning. He sighed and looked around. "Man, I wish I didn't have this job. I could use a night out with a couple of these girls. Oh well, back to work," he said to himself.

As a young unattached guy, Ben was able to play the scene well. He was also able to devote the time needed to research and develop his craft. A balance that could, at times, be difficult to handle. The coursework he took help things too. He was at the beginning of his career and just getting to know his way around the field. Ben thought with this case, he was on the verge of something big.

He checked over his notes to see if he had his facts together. As of now, there was something suspicious going on, but it wasn't the target that bothered him. To be honest, it was Mr. Taylor himself. Even though Preston had told him his father wanted to find out about this coworker, Ben thought it was important to check everyone involved. The information he found about Mr. Taylor didn't seem to coincide with anything Preston had said. This man, Walter, wasn't the one with a secret. It was Mr. Taylor who had some explaining to do.

Ben looked up to find Mr. Taylor walking toward him. He looked around to the left and right and took a seat with him. *Man, he doesn't look good*, Ben thought.

He had to rethink his strategy. *Should I tell him I know or not?*

"You said on the phone you needed to see me?" Robert looked at his son's friend. He seemed to be carrying the weight of the world on his shoulders. *What is it that he could have possibly found out about Walter?* Robert was sure he wouldn't have found anything. He guessed maybe he was wrong.

"Mr. Taylor," Ben started, "I have found out a couple of things, and I'm not sure how to proceed." He looked at Robert with his dark-chocolate eyes. His face was sad. He seemed to convey pity. *Interesting*, Robert thought.

"Well, tell me what is going on, and I may be able to shed some light on the situation." That was all Robert could say without giving too many details away. "I think I might be able to help out, but first please call me Robert."

Ben looked down and lifted an eyebrow and said, "OK." Then he opened the folder sitting in front of him and turned the laptop toward Robert. "Mr. Tay…I mean, Robert, I have not found anything to suspect Messenger has done anything deceitful in his past. He had a long-term relationship, but that has ended. In fact, she died. His brother, Jeff, lives in California. There is no other family listed on his records."

Robert didn't quite understand where his son's friend was going with this information. He decided to cut him off before he rambled anymore. "Ben, I don't understand. What you're telling me is great. Why do you look so concerned?"

It was then Ben let out a deep breath. He said, "Look, Mr. Taylor. I don't know or understand what you are looking for here. To be honest, I can't help but feel you have something more to tell me, and everyone else in your life."

This made Robert take notice. He sat up straight and stuttered, "Wh…wha…what do you mean? I have nothing to hide."

Ben wasn't surprised by Robert's reaction. He said, "I have your medical records. I make it a habit to know about everyone I'm investigating for and about. I know you're sick. The question is, does anyone else?"

The world began to tilt, and Robert didn't know which way was up. He needed to settle himself before he finished the conversation. He shook his head and stood, his angry face and hard stance appeared fierce. Ben started to say something, but Robert rejected Ben's statement. He scolded, "I didn't ask you to look into my background. I told you I wanted information regarding Mr. Messenger. Now if that's all, I'll be going."

Robert stood then said, "I expect your upmost professionalism here, Mr. Matthews." He dropped one thousand dollars on the table in front of Ben and with that stormed off.

Wow, Ben thought to himself. *That went…well.*

It was obvious that his illness was a sensitive topic for Mr. Taylor, and Ben would bet his PI license that no one else knew about his illness. It certainly seemed like it was something he wanted to keep to himself. Ben needed to figure out what to do, and quick.

17

Robert was in a complete and total panic. He didn't know what to do. If Ben told anyone, it would be the end to this charade. He looked at his watch. *Crap! I need to get to Schmidt's*, he thought to himself. He had to prepare for his meeting with Walter. He thought, hopefully, it would go better than the last.

As Robert got into his car, he picked up the phone to call his wife. He started to dial her number, but then he stopped. He thought to himself, *What on earth will I say to her?* He decided it was best not to call. He started the car and pulled out onto the road. The clock read 11:50 a.m.; he better move on so he could be there on time.

When he got to Schmidt's, he realized Walter was already there. He saw his Camaro parked out front of the restaurant. *Man, I wanted to be the first one here*, he said to himself. From a business standpoint, Robert felt this was key to having the upper hand. It was going to be him at the deficit today. Ever being the businessman that he was, Robert wasn't going to be at a disadvantage. He decided to hold his head up high and get what he wanted from this meeting.

The Schmidt's restaurant in German Village was hopping today. People were sitting in all nooks and crannies, talking about business or catching up on day-to-day life. Walter chose a table toward the back of the restaurant so he and Robert wouldn't be interrupted. He had great sight lines from his vantage point—a strategy he heard was key in negotiations. Walter needed to be on his toes when talking to Robert. He couldn't let his feelings for Alex get in the way. There was a difference in right and wrong, and the choices left to make.

Walter already felt terrible. He had to lie to Alex today so he could sneak off and meet with her husband. She was being lied to enough lately, and Walter hated being part of the problem. Usually they worked through lunch talking and laughing. It was imperative to get Julius's deranged idea out to the public. Today at lunch, however, he had to be on his own. He had a decision to make, and he hoped he made the right one.

The waiter swiftly dropped a cup of coffee in front of Walter before leaving to attend to other customers sitting nearby. He thought briefly about getting something a little stronger, but if he started drinking now, he wouldn't be able to stop. As he was taking a drink of his coffee, he realized Robert was walking into the restaurant. He signaled with a wave in Robert's way, and Robert walked toward him.

"Man, he doesn't look good," Walter said to himself. How in the world does he keep this from Alex? "Oh yeah, he doesn't come around," Walter whispered to himself while rolling his eyes. He hoped Robert didn't hear or see him, but at this point, he wasn't sure he cared. Alex was whom he cared about. Quite frankly, he couldn't understand these feelings he had for her, nor could he figure out how he had gotten himself into this situation. Walter was trying to wrap his head around it.

As Robert approached him, Walter stood to shake his hand. Robert seemed surprised by this action. He hesitated but then stuck his hand out for a hardy shake. Walter greeted him, "Hello, Mr. Taylor."

"Hello, Walter," Robert said. He took the seat across from Walter and placed the white linen napkin on his lap. He motioned to the waiter and ordered a Jack and Coke. Walter guessed by his choice of drink that this wasn't easy for Robert either.

"Mr. Taylor," Walter began, "I must tell you that you certainly put me into a difficult spot with your proposal."

Robert smiled. *He's smiling. Really, smiling?* Walter was baffled. Definitely not the reaction Walter thought the ill man should have at this point.

"First, please call me Robert. Secondly, I understand your point of view, and I can sympathize. But I have to tell you that my predicament is much more difficult than yours, I assure you."

He did have a point, but Walter wasn't ready quite yet to acquiesce. "Look, Mr. Tay—I mean, Robert, I have thought about this situation over and over, and I just can't see how either one of us possibly could benefit from this arrangement."

It was then Robert leaned forward and placed his elbows on the table. He sat his chin on upturned hands, almost in a prayer position. He took a deep breath and said, "It is not us that I am concerned with, Walter. It is my wife and kids. I will be leaving behind, as I stated before, a substantial sum. This money is for you to live on with my family. I expect you to use it that way."

Walter looked Robert straight into the eyes. Then he uttered, "What am I supposed to do? Move in to your house, sleep on your bed? You can't honestly believe that Alex would go for something like that, do you?"

He hadn't realized it, but his voice had steadily gotten louder. People around them quieted and looked their way. Robert started to wave his hands in a quieting motion toward Walter. He settled himself and quieted down. Robert took a swig of his drink. In his rant, Walter hadn't even noticed the waiter had set it down.

Finally, Robert said, "I never said it was going to be comfortable, Walter. Nothing worth having comes to anyone easily."

Robert noticed a difference in Walter's demeanor. Robert thought, *Good, he does have a feisty side!* This made Robert happy; his proverbial light turned on. He thought, *Now it's time to go in for the gold.* "Here is my plan. Listen to it and think about it before you decide. I think once you hear me out, you'll see why this is the best arrangement for you too."

18

There was a light at the end of the corridor, and Alex felt relief. She began to run as fast as her legs would take her, but she didn't seem to be getting any closer to the end. She screamed, "Come on! I have to get out."

No one was around to hear nor came to her aid. She decided she wasn't giving up. She'd run until her feet hurt or ran out of energy. It didn't matter. She seemed to have a sense of urgency. *Was Alex fighting for her life?*

At that point, Alex started to run at a faster pace. She kept running and running. Suddenly, a rock made her slip, and she landed on her knees. Tears started to fall. Alex couldn't hold back any longer. She sobbed and sobbed but to no avail.

Alex awoke in a deep sweat. The covers were completely wrapped around her, suffocating and stale. She was breathing heavily and totally dazed. She felt like a mummy stuck inside a tomb. *God, what was happening to her?*

It was late, and the moon was hanging like a beacon in the night. Robert was not home—again. "Enough is enough," she screamed.

Alex unrolled herself out from under the covers and threw them across the room. "Darn covers!" She slammed her feet on the ground and went stomping toward the closets. She grabbed a large suitcase and started pulling her husband's clothes off the rack, shoving them into the bag. At this point, she didn't care how they were packed. She just wanted to get anything associated with him out of her room.

She dragged the haphazardly packed luggage into the front room. By the time she got it all the way to the front door, she was huffing and puffing. She wiped the sweat from her brow and groaned. "I feel like the big bad wolf, but without the piglets."

As she grabbed for the doorknob, she heard the jingle of keys on the other side. She wasn't prepared for a face-to-face quite yet. She said, "Great! Now he wants to come home."

Then Alex said, "Well, too bad!" Not caring what she had on or who was behind the door, Alex ripped open the door. She yelled, "Now YOU FINALLY DECIDE TO COME HOME?"

⁂

Kayla was completely surprised by the state of her mother. From the looks of it, her mother was surprised to see her too. "Mom, what on earth is going on?"

Alex straightened and adjusted her nightgown. "I have no idea what you mean, dear."

Yeah, right! Kayla didn't believe her for one second.

"Where are you going, dressed like…*that*?" Kayla put emphasis on the last word. She was hoping to get her mother to realize she was partially dressed and not really in any state to go out.

"I'm not going anywhere, dear. It's your father. *He's going somewhere!*"

Kayla was completely puzzled. *What is going on? Where the hell is my father?* She asked, "Does this have anything to do with him being down at OSU Med Center a couple of weeks ago? Was he admitted there?"

Alex had no idea what was going on, but she was going to get to the bottom of it and quick! "I have no idea what you are talking about! What do you mean your dad was at the hospital?"

Kayla had to backtrack a little because she wasn't actually sure her dad had come to the hospital. She restated, "Well, I'm not sure it really was Dad, Mom. All I saw was a car that looked like yours and Dad's, but I never actually saw Dad."

Suddenly Alex started to cry. Through her sobs, she muttered, "I don't know, Kayla. Your dad's been odd lately." She was completely in hysterics now. Kayla reached out to her, but Alex didn't seem to notice. She continued, "He doesn't come home, and when he does, it's late at night or too early in the morning. I never see him at work, and when I do, he looks as if the weight of the world is on his shoulders, but he won't tell me a thing. I think there is someone else."

She took her mother's arm and guided her to the couch. She looked around for a tissue box but couldn't find one, so she went into the kitchen and got a paper towel. Her mother was sobbing uncontrollably, and Kayla was growing rather curious about what was going on with her parents. She brought the towel to her mother and said, "Let me make you some hot tea. Just leave the bag here and go get tucked in. I'll be in there in a couple of minutes."

When Kayla entered her parents' room, she found her mom asleep holding a wedding photo. For as long as Kayla could remember, it had been sitting on her mom's nightstand. She pulled the covers up and over her mom and pulled the photo from her grasp. Finally, she whispered in her mother's ear, "Mom, I'll try to find out what is going on. Don't worry yourself. Let me work on it. I love you." Lastly, she kissed her mother's forehead and turned to leave.

<hr />

The phone began to chime "Who Can It Be Now?" and Preston Taylor opened one eye. The light from his phone was too bright, so he closed it quickly. Then he groaned a loud "ugh!" When he looked at the clock, it was well past midnight. *Who in the world is calling me this late?* He didn't bother to open his eyes. Instead, he just slid his finger across the home screen and gave a guttural hello.

"Pres, it's Kayla." From the sound of her voice, she was obviously upset. This caused Preston to sit up and listen.

He was wide awake now. "Kayla, what's wrong?"

Kayla was glad she was able to reach her brother. She never knew what he was doing or whom he was doing it with.

"Kayla? Are you still there?" Preston couldn't help it, but he was growing a little agitated with his sister. He yawned and said with a wide-open mouth, "Look, Kayla, I'm really tired…"

Kayla didn't care how tired he was right now. She replied, "I'm worried about mom and dad, Preston," she implored. "I stopped by the house this evening, and mom was getting ready to kick dad out! She had his bags packed and everything."

Preston was sure his sister was exaggerating, but he couldn't help but put his confusion back into his voice too. "What are you talking about?" His head hurt already, and his mouth became dry. "I bet this has to do with Ben Matthews."

"*Ben?* Ben Matthews?" Kayla couldn't figure out what her brother's friend had to do with anything. "What are you talking about, Pres?"

Crap, did I say that out loud? Great, Pres. Nice going. Preston sighed. "Dad called me the other day and asked me to have Ben look up some new guy at work. He swore me not to tell anybody, but it just didn't seem quite right."

Kayla wondered what one thing had to do with another. She questioned her brother further, "Seriously, Preston, what in the world does that have to do with what I just said about mom?"

"Kayla, don't you see? Dad must think mom is the one having an affair with this guy! Did she mention him? His name is Walter something… Messenger, I think."

Kayla didn't back down. She said, "No! It's not Mom, Preston, it's Dad!"

Preston just didn't agree, but he continued to listen.

"Mom thinks Dad is the one having the affair! He's not coming home. He is leaving for work, and he's not taking her. Lately, he hasn't been answering her phone calls!" Kayla was out of breath. Preston could hear her heavy breathing on the other end.

He said, "I'm telling you, Kayla, it's Mom, not Dad." He was beginning to hate the fact that he answered the phone. He tried to calm her by saying, "Let me get with Ben and see what's going on. Let's not jump to any conclusions just yet."

Kayla couldn't let it go. She hadn't told Preston everything just yet but couldn't figure out if she wanted to tell him or not. He didn't seem to be listening. *He probably just thinks I'm being dramatic,* she thought.

To get her point across, she needed to tell him. She eased into it by saying, "Preston, I think Dad has been coming into the hospital. He has to be coming in to see Doc. I swear I saw him there the other day, but he slipped in and out of there before I got to talk with him."

She thought some more, then she carefully constructed her next sentence. She didn't want to alarm him, but she had to tell her brother the whole truth, or at least what she thought was the truth. She whispered, "I think Dad is sick."

"You have got to be kidding me! *Sick?*" a bewildered Preston said. "No way, our Dad is the picture of good health!"

It was then that Preston was done with the conversation. He couldn't actually believe Kayla was all worked up. He thought, *God, it isn't that big of a deal!* He continued, "I'm going back to sleep. You need to go to bed too." With that, he hung up the phone and went back to sleep.

When he awoke the next day, Preston decided he needed to get hold of two people, his friend and his father. He was going to get to the bottom of things. Even though he had dismissed his sister on the phone, he truly had to think on the points she raised. He hated to admit it, but Kayla was always more levelheaded. It was rare for her to speculate without good reason. He had to think more about what she had said on the phone. He couldn't help but smile. "I can't wait to hear what the two of them have to say," he whispered to himself.

19

Walter couldn't wait to see Alex today. He had thought about her all night long. After talking with Robert yesterday, he figured he needed to do his best to help Alex through whatever her husband was getting ready to inflict upon her and the family.

It was easy to support her as Robert wanted him to, but he was not going to overstep the bounds of friendship. For him, it all came down to his ethics. He couldn't be with a married woman, and he certainly wouldn't interfere in their relationship. *What can I do? Support her and be with her just like I know nothing?* Walter knew this would be a time of struggle for both of them.

He looked up and saw the jade eyes he loved so well staring right at him. Alex had just come off the elevator and was looking around with desperation. When she found him, she seemed to relax. Walter took in a deep breath and closed his eyes. He needed a pep talk before he actually spoke to her this morning. Unfortunately, when he opened his crystal-blue eyes back up, she was gone.

He didn't want to rush around to find her. He didn't want to seem desperate or too knowledgeable about what was going on. Walter stood and started to leisurely stroll to the vending area. He thought about getting a coffee then going to check in with his partner. He wanted to be nonchalant. *This is killing me.* He huffed. Of course it wasn't going to be that easy for him. She was calling to him like a beacon in the night.

☙❧

Alex was relieved to see Walter when she came into work this morning. She always appreciated how he was a consistent part of her life. At least one of the men in her life had some dependability. Unfortunately, she was on a mission once again to find her husband.

When Alex rounded the corner to her husband's office, she couldn't believe her eyes. Nothing resembling her husband was in there. All the pictures had been taken off the walls, and all the awards he had been given were gone too. *What in the world?*

Alex walked into the room in total panic. She looked in all of the drawers and the file cabinets. All of his files were there, but nothing personal.

A tear began to stream down her silken face. Just like at home, her husband's stuff was gone. Alex had hurried as fast as she could to get to the office. Once she had looked around, an instant feeling of dread hit her stomach. Almost everything relating to her husband was gone. There was nothing there to keep his presence alive. She didn't want to believe that her husband had left, but right now, there was no other reasonable thought. Once again, she sat down onto his chair in total defeat.

Alex was convinced this was all her doing. This was what she wanted after all. Once she started the process, she should have expected her husband to finish the job. He was always thorough in that way. She sighed. *He certainly showed me,* she chastised herself.

Tamara knocked on the door to Robert's office, startling Alex back into the present. Tamara saw Robert leave this morning with a box full of his belongings, but until now she hadn't put two and two together. "You OK?" she said to her best friend.

Alex looked at her friend and the kindness there. She said, "He's gone."

Tamara shook her head. She said, "I can see that, but why?"

Obviously, from the look on her face, Alex had no idea. Tamara figured there was someone else in Robert Taylor's life. It was the only thing that made sense at this time.

Alex said, "He's been building a different life for a few weeks now, or possibly months. I'm trying to figure it out now."

Tamara said, "I saw him this morning. He was carrying a box out with him. Honestly, I really didn't put two and two together." She hated how she could see her friend in despair. It was not a feeling she liked whatsoever.

"You saw Robert? *This* morning?" Alex said rather shocked. She must have just realized now that he had just been there this morning.

Tamara continued cautiously, "Yes. He didn't say anything to anybody. I'm surprised you didn't see him right before you came in. Didn't he walk right past you?"

The look of total confusion spread across Alex's face. She said, "You mean I just missed him!"

Tamara nodded at her friend in return. "I guess that's a no. Sorry, Alex, I didn't know."

Walter knocked on the door, and Alex looked up at him then quickly turned her head back down. He hated seeing that she couldn't face him, especially with tears running down her cheeks. She shielded her face in an effort to hide. Seeing her like this made his heart ache. He figured total embarrassment was the only thing that was keeping her in the spot she was now. Walter wanted to run right up to Alex and hold her in his arms. The total despair that was emanating off her was too much for him to take.

Sure he knew Robert was leaving, but he wasn't quite sure how it would go in the long run. Walter had asked him to keep him out of the details. He felt the little he knew, the better he was in playing the part.

"Alex, is everything OK?" It was all Walter could think to say, even though he knew perfectly well things probably would never be OK again for Alex.

Tamara looked over at him. She spit out a biting remark. "Does she look OK?" She was obviously irritated with all things male right now, but that didn't give her reason to be mean to him.

"I was talking to Alex," he said rather firmly.

Alex had obviously never heard him use such a tone with anyone; it showed on her face looking caught off guard. He said, "Alex, did you hear me? I saw Robert leave. What in the world is going on?"

Tamara was on point quickly. She said, "Walter, I'll take care of Alex. Why don't you go back to whatever it is you were doing?"

"I think I'd like to be here for her just as you are, Tamara. Thank you for your concern, but I'm more than caught up." Walter couldn't help but put the bite right back into his remarks. *Why was this lady on his case?*

"Enough!" Alex screamed between the two as she stood and slammed her hand on her husband's desk, his old desk. "Walter, I appreciate your thoughtfulness right now, but first I want to figure out what in the world is going on with my husband."

Alex then turned and looked at her friend. "Tamara, I'm not sure why you have such disdain right now for Walter. He isn't the one who's running out on his family to be with some… some…some Jezebel!"

Jezebel? Walter was puzzled. Then it dawned on him. *She thinks Robert is with another woman. Well now. Things are working out for Mr. Taylor.* Of course, he wasn't around to see the collateral damage. Walter was relieved in a way that Alex was angry at Robert, but then again, he felt like an opportunist too.

He looked at Tamara and nodded. He hoped to convey a she-told-you look. Then he heard Alex say, "Tamara, why don't you go and see if you can get a hold of Robert on his cell? I'm going to call my children and see what they may have heard. Walter, if you could just be around in case Julius calls, I'd certainly appreciate it."

Walter nodded and went to turn out of the office. He ran into Tamara as she was also going out the door. He tried to push through first, but together, neither one were able to go through. Walter wasn't giving any ground to this lady, and neither was Tamara. They each turned to the side and went through the door face to face.

Robert was breathing heavily. His head hurt, not to mention his heart too. It was just pure luck he barely missed Alex coming into the office this morning. He hated going into MCD and getting all of his personal effects. Robert knew he needed to do it to make his departure look authentic. Hopefully, he'd be able to get past this little road bump. He had to move on, although he did have a slight gleam of hope he'd return one day.

He was going to hop on a commuter flight and travel to the Cleveland Clinic. Doc had already set everything up for him, so he had nothing to worry about, so to speak. As he pulled his car into the long-term parking area, he laughed. *Ironic,* he thought to himself.

As he boarded the little commuter plane, he looked back, not quite sure what he was looking for. He was so used to having Alex and his children by his side that he felt out of sorts.

Robert realized a positive attitude may be the difference in getting through these treatments. *I chose this life. I need to persevere.* It might just be what he needed to get him a chance at a new life.

20

Kayla was waiting for Doc outside of the doctor's lounge at the OSU Medical Center. She was there to get some answers, answers she was sure Doc would have.

It had been a tough forty-eight hours since her father had gone missing. Her mother was a mess, holed up, and crying in her bed, not talking to anyone or eating anything. Kayla was beside herself with worry about both her parents. She had been sitting by her mother's side and rubbing her back, saying encouraging words. Kayla needed her mother back up and functioning soon. She needed to do it without her father too. *Damn him! Where was he?*

"Enough waiting," Kayla hastily said aloud. She stormed around the corner and down the flight of stairs. She wasn't going to give up easily.

As she walked down the hospital fairway, she couldn't help but stomp her feet. It was difficult to hold her temper. Then she examined the hospital vestibule and noticed her friend Laurie was working behind the desk.

As friends go, Laurie was top-notch. It was too bad her ex-husband was a loser. She had to work endlessly to take care of her kids. She certainly didn't want others to view her as vulnerable, but Kayla noticed her friend looked tired. Her highlighted blond hair was pulled back in a simple ponytail, and her lips were dressed up in bright red. She had a lot on her plate, but she still looked good.

"Hey, Laurie! How's it going?" Kayla smiled, but she was sure it didn't reach her eyes. It was hard to be happy when the weight of the world was on her shoulders.

Laurie Hays looked up and scrunched her eyes in a knowing look. She said, "Wow, girl. You looked stressed. What's up?"

Kayla tried to be calm and collected. She said, "I'm here to see Doctor Richardson. He has some forms I need. I have to have them to finish out my last course in nursing sciences." Kayla hoped her friend didn't realize she wasn't taking that class. She knew that at the hospital, you couldn't page a doctor just because you needed to find your daddy.

Her friend smiled almost knowingly. "Really, I didn't notice you in that class. I started taking it last week." She continued, "Come on, Kayla, tell me the truth."

Kayla started to stutter. "Well, I…I've been there. You must be taking it at a different time." She hoped it was convincing enough to settle her friend's curiosity.

Just then, the hospital's human resources director, Gina Meek, came off the elevator. Even though her position was considered rather prestigious, she always had been kind to Kayla and Laurie. Her short blond hair was highlighted in bright red. As it swayed, it seemed to glow under the fluorescent lights. She was lean and beautiful. Kayla always hoped she'd aged just like her dear friends.

When Gina walked up, she seemed to be able to read them both. "OK, girls. What's got you both so serious?" Just like that, she knew; her ESP amazed Kayla.

"Kayla needs Doc Richardson. Something about forms she needs filled out. Right, Kayla?" Laurie looked at Kayla and slightly nodded to encourage Kayla to answer.

Gina looked at Kayla and said, "Sorry, dear, he's on sabbatical. Is it something I can have one of the other doctors sign? Surely, I can help you out with whatever it is you need."

God, if only she could, Kayla thought to herself. *Now what am I going to do?* Her voice started hoarse but grew louder. "I really need him. Can you find him? *I need him!*" She was sure that her face showed complete and total panic. It was a feeling she was having a lot lately.

When Laurie saw Kayla's face went completely pale, she jumped into action. "Kayla, you have to tell us what's going on. You look as if you're going to pass out."

Kayla stared at the ground, her eyes getting bigger and bigger. She started to hyperventilate, and before she knew it, the world was engulfed with darkness. She hit the ground with a heavy thud, her friends looking on rather shocked.

৵৽ঌ

"What? Where?" Preston saw the hospital's number on his cell phone and immediately answered. He thought his mother had finally fallen over the edge of reason and sanity, but instead it was his sister.

A woman he had never met before was on the other end of the line. She continued, "Mr. Taylor, I'm Gina Meek. Kayla passed out here at the hospital when seeking to find Doctor Richardson. She seemed rather, uh, in an urgent need to talk to him. Unfortunately, he's on sabbatical right now."

All Preston could think about was how lucky his big sister had been to be at the hospital. *For the love of Pete, I told her to stay out of it!* He had to think on his feet here, and quick. *First, I'll go and check on her. Then, I'll KILL her!*

The woman on the other end was not privy to his thoughts. She asked, "Mr. Taylor, are you there?"

He responded to her with a calm "I will be right there." Hanging up the phone, he practically ran out the door. Preston needed to get to his sister, and quick.

ॐ

Robert sat at the other end of the conference table as his friend of many years sat beside him. He was looking and feeling pretty bad and couldn't help but think it was only a matter of time before he passed away.

Unfortunately, Doc had taken a sabbatical to keep his plans with Robert on the down-low. It wasn't something he was convinced to do easily. Robert had to coax him, but in the end, it worked. Doc had finally realized it was the best for everyone involved.

Robert heard a sigh come from the man. He swore he heard him say, "I needed those days too." *What was he thinking about?* Robert's head cocked to the side. He said, "I'm sorry, did you say something?" Doc just looked at him, but he didn't say anything at all.

At this time of the day, not many people were in the Toronto-based medical center known for the use of state-of-the-art technology and top endocrinologist care. The Cleveland Clinic had the doctor they were going to see. She was one of the newest and brightest stars in the field. Even though Doc was considered a foremost professional, he always told Robert he wasn't shy on seeking out help at any time.

The door to the conference room opened, and one of the most exquisite creatures Robert had ever seen walked through the door. Standing nearly six feet tall and all legs, Camille Rini was a force to be reckoned with. Her beautiful red hair was pulled back tightly in a bun, little wisps of it framed her face. She had a silver ballpoint pen shoved inside her bun.

Looking from her head to her feet, Robert was completely blown away. Her blue eyes were a stark contrast to the white lab coat she had on. He'd never seen a redhead with blue eyes before. *Wow*, he thought.

Doc smiled at the young lady then stood up to shake her hand. He looked at Robert and raised his eyebrows. Robert realized he needed to do the same thing. He stood and stuck out his hand as Doc introduced him to her.

"Doctor Rini, this is Robert Taylor." He looked at Robert then back at the doctor. Then he said, "Robert, this is Doctor Rini."

The young knockout didn't look Robert's way at first, so Robert put his hand down. She squealed, "How nice it is to see you, Doctor Richardson! What has it been, at least six months?" She looked at the portly man and gave him a big hug. Doc blushed and smiled. Robert knew the feeling; he was flustered just looking at her.

Finally she turned to Robert. She smiled then said, "Mr. Taylor, please call me Dr. Camille. All my patients do."

He nodded and said, "Dr. Camille it is then."

Robert stuck out his had one more time. He smiled and was again surprised by her stunning beauty. Electricity seemed to flow between them when they connected hands. Her sultry eyes turned his resolve head over heels. Then he remembered he was married.

21

"What do you mean you had a meeting with my dad before he went missing?" Preston could not believe his ears. His friend had information. *Dammit,* he thought, *why hadn't he said something before?*

Suddenly Preston was angry. He scolded, "It's been three months. You mean you are just now getting to tell me this? I can't believe this, Ben, I've been asking you since day one."

Ben seemed to hesitate. Preston wasn't sure how he was going to respond, but he couldn't wait to hear his friend's excuse.

Ben replied, "Look, Preston, I'm not supposed to be telling you these things. Your dad was my client, and I do have some responsibility to him here."

"*Responsibility?*" Preston couldn't gather his words because of the hurt settling in his stomach. He began to stutter, small sounds came pouring out of his mouth. He took a deep breath. Then he was able to finish his thought. He said, "Response…responsibility? *Are you kidding me?* Ben, I've been your friend for years. Don't you have some obligation to me too?"

He wasn't finished, but he had to pause as tears started to form in the corner of his eyes. He whispered, "Help me here, *please*."

Preston hoped his friend could see what was right in this situation. Ben had to understand his point of view. Preston knew his friend had more details, important details he needed to help him find his father. In fact, he was counting on it!

Ben said, "Look, man, I truly don't think there was anything wrong with the target he had me research."

Preston heard shuffling in the background. He assumed Ben was looking at some sort of papers or files.

He went on, "The guy, Walter Messenger, he seemed like a stand-up guy with a solid background. Interestingly enough, it wasn't what I found out about him that puzzled me. Preston, I hate to say this, but your father's status was more alarming."

Preston didn't understand. *God, not him too. First Kayla, now Ben.* Preston asked, "My father's status, what do you mean? Why would you look up info on dad too?"

"Standard procedure. I try to have all of my bases covered should something happen between the two parties, and I need to get that info to the authorities. Ya know? Anyway, the most interesting thing I found out was that…your dad was ill."

Kayla had been right. She'd tried to convince him, but he just hadn't listened. Well, he was listening now. He had so many questions for his friend. He probed, "Ill with what exactly?"

"Your dad was diagnosed by a Doctor Richardson about a month or so before he went missing. He was receiving treatments at OSU too. I don't get it, man, didn't he tell you all of this?"

"No, he didn't," Preston said.

Preston finished his conversation with Ben. He hung up the phone with new determination. He was going to find out exactly who knew his dad's little secret. He knew exactly the person he needed to see first.

In the three months since Robert had disappeared, Walter had done everything he could to support Alex and her kids. To be honest, he was loving every minute with his newfound family.

❦

Walter knew deep down it was all a lie. He knew exactly where Robert was, at least he thought he did. The incredible guilt, however, sent him over the edge. Alex was losing weight; she wouldn't eat a thing. Her kids were trying to help, but he knew they weren't going to find out anything. Robert made sure of that. The day was turning out pretty beautiful, and he had taken an early run. The run had helped to clear his mind.

Once he had gotten ready for work, he headed to the garage to pick up his Camaro. As he sat down on the driver's seat, his cell phone rang. Walter noticed Preston's number on the home screen. Since his father had gone missing, Preston had seemed to latch on to Walter. He had grown fond of Preston too. He was a good young man with a big heart.

On a daily basis, the newfound friends would touch base with each other to see how Alex had been feeling. Walter answered, "Hey, Preston. What's up?"

"Walter, are you with my mother?" Preston blurted out.

Instantly, Walter was on alert. "No, bud. I'd think she'd be at work. I haven't made it in yet. Is everything OK?"

Preston responded, "I need to speak with her…and you. Are you going into MCD now?"

Interesting, Walter thought. *This is a little out of the ordinary.* Maybe he needed to get a little more information. "Sure am, but I need to meet up with Julius, I mean, Mr. Whinehart today."

He began searching for his date book in his briefcase. As he looked, Walter continued, "Let me look at my schedule and get back with you. Is there an emergency? If there is, I can open up some time, man."

"It's important, but I really need Mom too. I spoke with a friend of mine just now. His name is Ben Matthews. Remember him? He's been working on helping us find Dad. I think he has something we all need to hear."

Alex had mentioned a friend of her son's in passing, and the mention of him made Walter's ears perk up. This kid, well, man, was a PI. He had been working on discovering new leads on Robert's case.

For Walter, Ben Matthews was a wild card in this whole situation. Unfortunately, he hadn't known about Ben's background at first. Robert had failed to mention this in his "plan." He realized it was time to get in touch with the man himself. This "friend," Walter suspected, could potentially become a problem, a *big* problem.

When Preston finished, Walter found his planner. He thought about it for a moment and realized he needed to deflect him for a little while so that he could get in touch with Robert. He hated to do it, but he had to lie to Preston. He said, "Sure... Oh, I must not have taken my planner home. Let me get into the office and check in with your mom. Sound good?"

"OK, that sounds good." Preston seemed reluctant but went along with it anyway.

"Great! I'll call you in about a half hour." With that, Walter disconnected.

A little while later, just as he had witnessed the good and bad guys do in the movies, Walter purchased a disposable phone. He heard it was the only kind that couldn't be traced and could subsequently be thrown away. Although a little dramatic, he felt like a criminal trying to cover up a crime. *The guilt*, Walter thought. *It's got to be the guilt.*

Being raised Christian, Walter always believed in a higher power, and he tried to uphold the teachings he learned as a child. The problem was, Walter couldn't figure out how to balance his beliefs and his newly confessed love for Alex. He wasn't able to deny either anymore.

Once he had bought the phone, he couldn't actually dial it. Walter had the hospital's number for over a week. He kept it in his pocket, and like the saying goes, it was burning a hole there. He stuffed the number back in his pocket along with the phone. Calling would have to wait until later. Now he had to think.

Things had grown quite comfortable between him and Alex. She seemed to light up in his presence. The smiles were coming more easily, and the laughs becoming more frequent. These sounds Walter strived to hear every single day. It made his heart skip a beat.

He walked along a city block of the Short North looking into the numerous store windows but not really seeing anything at all. He knew his time with Alex was coming to a close. Once he convinced her husband to return, he'd leave and go back to California, the only outcome he could conceive doable at the time. Walter turned around and headed back to his car. He had to get into MCD. He had to see Alex, and quick.

22

Alex stared out her office window, looking at a beautiful and bright day in the capital city. She wished her mood mirrored the weather outside. She had been counting the days since she last saw her husband, ninety-two days so far, and she was feeling like anything but sunshine. The ache in her heart was cumbersome to her withering-away frame. She hadn't eaten, not slept a full night, or been able to get much work done, to say the least.

Trying to live on the positive side, however, Alex was thankful that she had beautiful children and a new friend in Walter. He had been spending a lot of time with her, and Alex couldn't deny her feelings for him anymore. Strength emanated off him, and Alex sucked it up like a plant seeking out light to nourish its growth.

Walter had been stopping by to see her on the weekends and visiting her and her children on a regular basis each and every week. They had fallen into quite the routine, like a little family. The irony was not lost on Alex.

A sound of knocking brought Alex's attention back to the present. She acknowledged the visitor by saying, "Come in." She was surprised that her assistant had been

Mixed Emotions

waiting on the other side of the door. Normally Albert wouldn't have bothered with this proper office etiquette. In fact, he usually drove her bonkers and barged into wherever he wanted.

"Alex," he said rather meekly. "You have a visitor, and I think you might want to sit down."

Puzzled, she turned her head to the side. Not thinking, she looked down and picked up her mail from the office. She had just begun to open it but stopped. She could smell him before she could see him; she'd know that scent anywhere. Her husband. He was finally home.

✧

Robert was astonished at how much weight his wife had lost. He never dreamed she would have taken his leave so hard. He was trying to save her the heartache, but obviously, his intentions were mute. As she looked at him with her piercing green eyes, he smiled and went to give her a hug. It was a feeling that came to him on a whim. He'd thought about what he needed to do the whole way home from Canada. Hugging was not one of them.

Suddenly an object flew past Robert's head. It snapped him into his present reality, and he stopped dead in his tracks! He looked around to see what his wife had actually thrown at him. It wasn't hard to find since the evidence was stuck into her office door. "Alex, honey. You threw a letter opener at me!" Surprise was evident in his voice.

Alex's face was a bright red now. Words full of venom began to follow out of her mouth. "Honey? You leave for three months and you call me HONEY!"

Robert cringed as Alex screamed across the office at him. She certainly was rather upset. He'd expected that. In fact, he actually thought she had taken it quite well. Suddenly the door came swinging open, smashing the backside against the wall and pushing the tip of the letter opener further through the front too. The next thing he knew he was crashing toward the ground. A rather large force had come barreling into the room. Unfortunately, Robert had gotten the full brunt of the hit.

Walter was in panic. He had heard yelling and a rather large bang come from Alex's office, and he took off in a sprint. Something had happened in her office, and he was going to find out what it was.

He passed by a wide-eyed Albert and threw open the door. He didn't expect the gold-tipped letter opener pushing through, so he had to tuck and roll to get into her door unscathed. Unfortunately, he managed to take down the person standing behind the door too. When he looked at the poor victim to his grand entrance, he was aghast at whom he saw.

"What in the world?" he whispered to himself. Robert. He never thought he'd see him again. He actually *hoped* he never saw him again. The words started pouring out, "Robert, you look…healthy! Are you OK? Where in the world have you been?"

Robert stood and started to brush himself off. He didn't bother to stick a hand out for Walter, a point that wasn't missed by him. Walter stood too. He instantly went over to stand beside Alex; by the look on her face, she might have killed Robert if he didn't.

"Walter, I had a feeling I'd see you today. At least that's what I expected, per our agreement." Robert's eyes were trained on him as he spoke. Then he looked at Alex.

Alex stared at her husband and then at her friend. She looked back at Robert again. What had Robert just said—an agreement? She turned her tear-filled eyes at Walter. "Walter, what is he talking about?" The devastation was thick within her words.

Robert began to explain, "Walter and I had discussed a few months ago an arrangement. Doc diagnosed me with pancreatic cancer, and I wanted you to be taken care of while I was away getting treatment."

Alex's face whipped around to look straight at her husband. "Taken care of? I'm your WIFE, not a DOG!" She was screaming, her normal cream-colored skin a bright red, Rudolph red, once again. "You can't leave for three months without any word or letter or e-mail for God's sake. I've been worried sick, and your kids have gone out of their minds looking for you too!"

She continued, "And you"—she rounded on Walter—"you agreed with him! You *knew* what he was doing?" She looked at him again as she began to sob. "You... knew?"

The devastation was virtually dripping off her. It nearly broke him. Walter said quietly, "Alex, I was going to tell you, today in fact. I was going to call him today and tell him enough was enough!"

Robert took a breath. "Actually, Alex, it was you and the kids I was thinking most about. I didn't know what was going to happen, but I thought I was going to die."

"Robert, that's my job. I'm your wife. Don't you understand?" Alex was firm in her resolve, and Robert was taken aback.

Walter went to say something, but Alex threw up her arm to stop him. She said, "Why did you agree to this?"

She stormed past both of them and out the door. She turned around to say something else but just didn't seem to have the words. Alex was defeated, and Walter completely understood.

Robert watched as his wife walked out the door. He then faced his replacement and began to speak, "Walter, I asked you to take care of Alex. Obviously, I shouldn't have depended on you for this job."

Walter was sad and devastated all in the same breath. He questioned Robert's words. "You're kidding me, right? You leave, wreck lives, and then come back as if nothing has happened at all."

Robert wasn't at all affected by Walter's words. He said, "Walter, I did what anyone would do in this situation. I took care of the issues at hand. You are in this just as much as I am. From now on though, this will be your place. I'm here for a divorce."

23

"A divorce?" Walter couldn't believe what Robert had just said. He murmured, "You came back here for a divorce?" These words should have made Walter feel like he was on top of the world, but he wasn't. He felt lower than low.

"Isn't that what you want?" Robert asked Walter.

Was it? Right now, Walter didn't know. All he could think about was attending to Alex. "Robert, she's been worried sick about you. She hasn't been eating, nor has she been sleeping. I've worked side by side with her for the past ninety-some days, and she has been devastated. If I were you, I'd think about that. She loves you, not me."

Walter left Alex's office and went in search for her. It should be her husband going to look for her, not him. That point wasn't lost on him. Robert didn't even move when Walter left. This made him more suspect to what Robert was actually doing here.

He walked through the hallways and even searched through the restrooms. Alex wasn't anywhere. Where would she have gone? That was when he began thinking about the rooftop lookout. Maybe, just maybe, she might be there.

Standing on top of MCD, Alex saw an airplane taking off from Port Columbus International Airport. She watched as it gained altitude and wished she was on that plane, even if she didn't know where it was going.

Then she turned her attention to the town below. Cars of all different shapes and sizes darted in and out of traffic. Various types of people walked to and from their offices. Businesses were humming with sounds. No one seemed to have a care in the world.

Only a few months ago, one might have observed Alex the same way. But now, her thoughts were whirling around just as the wind she felt flowing through her hair. At first, Alex couldn't help but feel relief. She knew her husband was alive and safe too. Sure she was mad at him, but she had heard his plea. He thought he was dying. This didn't excuse his behavior, however. Nothing could have excused this behavior. Alex thought, *Why wouldn't he have trusted me with this information?*

Then her thoughts turned to Walter. She found it rather ironic that she was at this point again. Hadn't she just been having this same conversation with herself in the office just an hour before? Ever since Walter came into her life, he had been there for her. He had never pressed her for anything, nor had he been expecting anything from her either.

Alex heard a loud creak and bang behind her. It was the sound of the building door opening and closing, she was sure of it. She didn't turn around though. She didn't care who it was or what they wanted. A shadow formed on the wall, and a figure came to stand next to her. She looked over to find Walter. Interestingly enough, Alex was shocked to see him. She knew she shouldn't have been surprised, but she was. Then her heart ached. She wondered, *Why wouldn't my husband have come to find me?*

Alex didn't say anything. She just stood in a comfortable silence with Walter. Then she heard him take in a deep breath. He had something to say, and it must be important. Obviously, he was choosing his words. She didn't make him suffer any longer. She quizzed him, "What is it, Walter?"

⁂

Walter shouldn't have been surprised that she knew he needed to say something. Alex was good at reading people that way. "Alex, I'm sorry. Truly sorry." He hoped she believed him; he was being sincere. "Robert came to me worried about you. He was sick. Cancer, he said, and he was worried about you and the kids."

"Worried about me and the kids?" Alex was not convinced. "Walter, he left us. I thought he was dead. Do you have any idea how that feels?"

"Actually, I do." The words came out meek. He didn't want to open this wound again, but he had to for Alex.

Alex was confused. "What?"

"I was almost engaged once."

This was news to her. Walter had never mentioned it before, and it obviously was painful for him to share now. A strange tingle of jealously hit Alex's heart; this was a feeling that surprised her too. She groaned. *They were all full of surprises today.* Finally, Alex said, "You never mentioned it before. Why now?"

Walter put his hand on her arm and turned her toward him. She looked up at him with those beautiful green and glowing eyes. He briefly saw the face of his old girlfriend flash before him. He shook his head, bringing him back to the present.

Alex seemed confused. She cocked her head slightly to the side, as if waiting for him to say something. He began to tell his story. "It was in college when I met a beautiful girl named Shannon King. She was a feisty coed, with as beautiful set of green eyes, and just the slightest bit of sarcasm that always made me laugh."

He paused for a minute then continued once again. "We had been together for a while, and everything was going beautifully. I knew in my heart I wanted her to be my wife, so on Christmas Eve that year, I proposed. She said no, and I was stunned. She just said no."

A tear started to slide down his cheek. Alex lifted up on her toes and wiped it with her small hand. Walter put his hand on top of hers and leaned onto it. She said, "Then what happened?"

"I don't know, really. I just came home one day to find her peacefully resting in our bed. There was a note beside her. It told me how she loved me and she was sorry, but life for her was coming to an end. She was ill too. Cancer." Walter's hurt shone through his eyes. His voice wavered a little then he said, "She wasn't just resting there, Alex. She was dead."

Alex was dumfounded. She couldn't believe she was just hearing this for the first time. Here she was being so selfish, and he was aching inside. She was ashamed. "Oh Walter, I didn't know. You must think I'm such a selfish person. Standing up here moping when my husband is downstairs alive and…*well*."

"That's just the point, Alex, I don't. I would probably feel the exact same way in your situation." Although confused by his own feelings for her, he said, "I'm not sure what the future will hold, but I just want you to know I'm here for you. I love you, Alex." With that, he bent down and kissed the tip of her nose, then he turned around and walked away. All Alex could do was watch him go. She was too stunned by his declaration to move from her spot.

24

Six months had passed since that day on the rooftop, and many things in Alex's life had changed. For one, Robert's diagnosis had turned out to be inaccurate. He confessed to her that being gone those few months had been as difficult on him as it was for their family, but his doctor had assured him he needed a "mental health" break. In addition, he guaranteed he would stay, all the while saying he'd love her until the end of time. Unfortunately, this reappearing act didn't hold. Robert had gone again, professing his love for someone else not but two months later. Ironically, her husband had fallen for that same doctor who prescribed him those months of "treatment." *Treatment, my butt,* Alex thought.

It wasn't that Alex hadn't tried to reason with him. She told him it was merely the Nightingale effect, but here she sat on her empty king-size bed, having received the divorce papers just the day before Christmas. Her heart was hurting, and it was hurting bad. "Merry Christmas to me," she said to herself.

Alex wasn't the only one who was hurt by Robert again; their children were too. She was sure neither of them had spoken one word to him since he said he was leaving again. Since the holidays were approaching, she encouraged them to at least give him a call. Both of them had been devastated when they thought he was dead, but Alex was sure if they didn't try harder to mend that relationship, they would regret it. Sure, mending relationships weren't that easy, but it was necessary. As a way to ease their pain, she repeatedly reminded them that at least he said good-bye this time. A thought that usually came across loudly but fell upon deaf ears with little to no response from their children.

Alex hadn't even mentioned the fact that their father was divorcing her. Being the holidays and all, she didn't think it was appropriate. As their mother, she wanted to make the holidays as enjoyable as possible. Even if he didn't feel that way for her. She made her way over to the master bathroom and took a shower to prepare for the festivities. Alex fixed her hair and makeup just right, an activity she hadn't bothered to do in quite a while, but today she wanted to look her best when everyone arrived. She even pulled out one of her favorite red dresses as a way to make herself feel better too. It certainly helped to lift her spirits over the gloomy feelings she had earlier today.

※

The glittering fresh snow caught Alex's attention as she briefly looked out the kitchen window. The meal her family would enjoy was cooking in the oven and simmering on the stove. Alex realized the children would be there soon; it was time to prepare the mashed potatoes. She heaved a heavy sigh thinking that mashed potatoes had been her husband's favorite. Pushing that thought aside, she grabbed all of the ingredients and started to peel the potatoes. Once complete, she proceeded to place each one carefully into the pot of boiling water.

Everything seemed to be going as planned. Alex looked at the clock and noticed it was time for the evening news. She just needed a little background noise. The house was too quiet right now, and she felt too alone. She made her way over to the TV, turning it to channel 10; with any luck, she may catch the story about the project she had worked on with Walter all those months before. She walked back over to the stove and turned down the heat. To her relief, she had just caught the water in mid-foam before it began to boil over the sides. *Thank goodness,* she thought to herself. *I don't need to make a mess of things before we even get the night underway.*

Suddenly, the jingle for the news came over the airways. She smiled at the banter both the anchormen and women began speaking back and forth to one another. Then the weatherman made his report, and from what he said, it seemed the snow was going to continue. Alex responded to the man even though he couldn't hear, "Good, snow on Christmas. I love it when it snows. At least something right is going on around here."

Alex continued to work, putting on her oven mitts to remove the potatoes off the stove. As she held the pot in her hand, the team of reporters returned for breaking news. Alex paused a moment to hear the speaker; she was midstep when the reporter began to speak on location.

"This just in! The Japanese company responsible for the geisha Barbie has filed for Chapter 13 bankruptcy today. A spokesperson for the production company could not be reached at this time. As you may remember, the advertising firm that brought this eastern sensation to us is located right here in Columbus. We were on location earlier today, and here is our report."

The screen then flashed to the outside of MCD, LLC and then inside the lobby. The reporter continued, "We arrived here at MCD, LLC earlier today after rumblings began to stir about the impending financial trouble for the once formidable Japanese company, Lawsonamto and Currbolinsaki."

"What in the world?" Alex didn't remember seeing any reporters today. Not knowing what was happening made her uncomfortable. In actuality, she was beside herself. She had no idea this was going on. The Japanese company had made millions when the doll was introduced to the United States. Alex thought Julius must be livid wherever he is. But then again, the agency had made its money, so why would he care at all?

Alex shrugged her shoulders and turned to proceed with cooking. She didn't really pay much attention to what was said by the reporter right after that. She figured it had to be more on what the press had been told thus far, and nothing that would pertain to her anymore.

As she had just about gotten the pot of potatoes to the counter to begin whipping them with a mixer, she spotted a familiar face profile out of the corner of her eye. Then she heard the familiar timber of a voice beginning to speak. "We here at MCD are saddened by the news that our business partner has suffered such a great loss."

Walter? She must be dreaming. She whispered, "Could it really be true?"

The world started to tilt, and the pot of potatoes slipped out of Alex's hands. As the pot hit the floor, hot potatoes exploded everywhere, including on Alex. She couldn't help but scream as the starchy vegetable landed all over her legs and dress. It burned, and as she looked down, it was everywhere! She shouted, "FUDGE! Of course this would happen today!"

Alex slid down to the floor after frantically looking around the room for a towel. She needed to clean herself off as well as wipe the floor. As the pain of each little burn set in, tears of hurt poured down her face. She vigorously wiped everything within her reach. She'd worry about herself in a minute.

Suddenly, Alex noticed smoke billowing out of the stove. She yelled, "CRAP! The ham!" She stood up, sliding just a little on a fragment of potato still left on the ground and grabbed the handle to open the oven. The smoke was too heavy and made Alex choke. She reached inside for the pan of ham and ran toward the front door. As she opened it to toss the ham outside, it launched from her hands just seconds before she realized someone was standing in the direct line of fire.

༺❦༻

Walter noticed the billowing smoke then the flying ham coming toward his head. He had just enough time to duck before it smacked him in the face. Unfortunately, this meant he didn't have solid enough footing to catch Alex on her way out too.

Both of them landed in a snow pile to the left of her porch. Walter rolled so he could take the brunt of the fall. As he came to a stop on his back, he couldn't help but notice the mashed potatoes dripping off her hair. She looked startled and overwhelmed all at the same time. Walter smiled. Leave it to Alex to make a grand entrance as always.

"I usually like my ham a little less burnt and my potatoes on a plate. But for right now, I'll take them any way I can have them," Walter said jovially. Alex's green eyes were pinned on him, and her mouth was hanging open. Suddenly she started violently coughing, and Walter sat up and pulled her on his lap. He patted her back and rocked her back and forth. He was so happy to have her in his arms. He always knew he'd love having her in his arms. He whispered, "Shh, sweetie. It's OK. Do you need me to call the fire department?"

The coughing subsided, and Alex smiled. She wrapped her arms around Walter's neck and hugged him as hard as she could manage. Alex released Walter and sat back to look at him. She couldn't help herself. She just had to fire a feisty comment right back at him. "I think the fire is out on the inside of the house. But I have to say, I'm beginning to think food of any kind is bad for my health."

Walter just smiled. Then he said, "Well, maybe from hereon out, I'll be the cook."

Alex thought that was an excellent idea.